STUCK ON *You* 2

A NOVEL BY

SUNNY GIOVANNI

From Sunny...

Sometimes we have to walk through the fire after we're forced to leave the one we love for someone or something else, and sometimes we have to wander through darkness before we finally make it to the light. Two years ago, I was a witness to this. I had a woman break me down so badly that, for two weeks straight, I couldn't eat, sleep, focus and write. I remember calling my best friend to drag her into my lair, so that she could see what kind of hell I had been living in. Yet, I wasn't innocent. It was only so much that this woman could take before she gave me what I had given her. I was a monster. My mouth was slick, and my intentions were evil. Whereas I didn't physically abuse her, it was more mental and emotional. No, I didn't realize it. She was a damn good one, too, so there was no reason to do some of the things I did. That old saying of how you don't know what you have until it's gone is true. Then something else hit me. As I rose from the ashes of my own destruction, it donned on me that I had a good one long before her, only I hadn't paid attention to it. So then came the reconstruction. If I was going to be in another relationship, I was determined not to be the same ugly person that I was before. My own best friend had always been on the forefronts since we were thirteen years old, and I never really realized how much of a soldier for me that she was. Witnessing everything that she had gone through was sickening. I saw a bit of my ugly self in almost every person that she'd dated. That was my cue to step in and claim what was rightfully mine. In honor of the woman that I tore down and the hearts that I had broken prior to her, I made a deal with myself that if I championed my own best friend, that I would make her happy for the rest of her days. Fourteen years of friendship to this very date of release, and finally, we're home. Together. Hand in hand. Happy. No pain. No suffering. No lies. No tension. No discombobulation. You really don't know what you have until you open your eyes, ladies and gentlemen. Yea, it took us fourteen years to get here, but there was a lot of war in between time, but we're finally home. A new me. A new her. Beautiful. I've learned to love me before I could love someone else, and my issue was that I had a mountain of insecurities when I was with the other woman, which reflected in mental and emotional abuse. It was wrong. Very wrong. I still kick my own ass over it, so I don't need judgement and ridicule. But it helps to know that she's finally happy and snagged her happily ever after. All of this to say that love is not easy, but if you're willing, you'll put on your big girl or big boy undies and do what needs to be done in order to reach your happiness. Love, live and build.

Gio, out.

PROLOGUE

11 Years Ago...

*S*hane was the first out of the school, and that was only because he skipped his last period's course. Patiently, he waited out front near the bike racks as he ran his fingers through the parts of his twists with his thin binder tucked underneath his arm. Apollo didn't tolerate his afro, so he made him get twists instead because they were neater and more presentable to him.

Rich came out second and dapped him up. "Waitin' on Rie?" he asked him as he scanned the swarming bunch of young teens for something pretty and easy.

"You know it," Shane chuckled, until his smile faded into a frown. He had to remember that she was gone. He was stuck in a routine of what used to be. She had been gone for all of two weeks now, and he couldn't get over it. "You gon' be at Ms. Pat's today?" he asked, trying to change the subject.

"Maybe... maybe not." Rich failed to meet Shane's eyes yet, but everyone knew that with the way Rich was built, he never sat still for long anyway, so what was the point in looking at someone? "I'ma check you later though, scab. I gotta catch up with somebody."

Shane slapped five with him and let his friend go his separate way.

Mandy slapped the back of his shoulder and placed her hand on her hip.

He turned to face her with a grimace. "Girl, what the hell? You want to get hit back?"

"Boy, shut up! You comin' by my house today?"

"Maybe. Rich ain't gon' be there, and I don't want to be the only one there with you."

"Whatever, Shane. Just leave me to be bored then! Y'all ain't nothin'! Just because my cousin left, it doesn't mean that we aren't friends."

"Amanda Bama Bananas... I'm sorry." He grinned and reached for her hand.

She snatched it away and rolled her eyes. "One day, you gon' miss me, De'Shane. One dang-on day."

"I already miss you, baby." He placed his hands over his heart and blew her a kiss.

In return, she shot him the middle finger.

His cellphone vibrated in his pocket, and he cautiously reached in to answer. Living in his new home with his new dad still hadn't gotten the better of him, and he had yet to get used to it.

"Yes, sir," he said humbly when he answered.

"You know I can see you, right?" Apollo asked him.

Shane whipped his head from left to right, then whirled around to the street to finally spot the stretch Navigator along the curb.

"Let's go. You ain't got time to stand around and play with your friends. De'Shane is becoming a man. He has to go to work."

"Yes, sir," he replied before hanging up.

Apollo crossed his legs with his cane at his side. He was thoroughly impressed at how well Shane had been taking his move and the transition. What he didn't know was that it was all on the outside, because inside Shane was disheveled. He was close to breaking at the thought of losing everything he once knew. He only put on a good front for the sake of his father.

Apollo had taken him by the nursing home to see Michelle, where Shane held on to his tears pretty well, and only excused himself once to go to the restroom to try and get rid of himself. This was not what he wanted, and it felt like he was screaming and no one was listening. When he returned, Michelle complimented him on how his lineup was fresh, he was standing straight up, and how his twists looked much better than what she called his nappy and uneven afro. He rustled a smile for her and left the room with his chin in the air, so that he wouldn't get whacked with Apollo's cane.

Once they were inside Apollo's limo, Shane stared out of the window, and the only thing that reflected on it was the $2,000 earrings in his ears. Once upon a time, Shane would've only imagined having so much money so close. Now he was living a dream and a nightmare. Being the son of a kingpin wasn't easy. Especially when he had no one who he could talk to, to help him through the transition. That girl who was unbiased to everything was out there somewhere, and he only prayed that she would come back.

Apollo had his driver to pull into the warehouse, so Shane could finally work. It was considered his chore. He had received a new shipment, and he needed the boy with as much talent as he had to put it to use.

Shane got out of the Navigator and stuffed his hands into the pockets of his heavily creased black pants, after popping the collar of his black, starched button up. Then, he casually strolled into the warehouse, feeling like he had a chain around his neck. Bo led him to a table while shouting orders at men who were moving boxes around out of delivery truck. When Bo stopped, Shane looked at the bricks on the table and tapped his finger on his leg to calculate.

"Twenty-two bricks," Shane blurted as he moved around the table so that he could calculate the money in his head. His eyes were swaying from left to right to get all of his numbers and figures together. "If it's twenty-two bricks on each table, and there are..." He looked up and spun around for a minute until he had the math down. "...eight tables. If eight tables by twenty-two bricks is 176 bricks even. That's 177,480 keys. Dad, your keys go for fifty bucks a pop... that's..."

Apollo squeezed his cane, on edge like the rest of the workers who had stopped to hear how quickly Shane could calculate once more. He might as well had been the Boy Wonder with his talent.

"That's... 887 million... with 400 left over for chump change," Shane miserably concluded.

Bo squeezed his brows together. Something was wrong in the

prince's tone.

Shane spun around a few more times until he figured out where he had gone wrong. He wasn't confident in his answer. He was missing something.

Apollo kept his eyes on his kid.

Shane walked the rows of tables and paced between three of them, almost scarring up his new patent leather Jordan's, until he stopped and eyed the cocaine on the table in front of him. "You're missing four bricks!" he announced. "That's not right," Shane panicked. "You… you don't like uneven work on your tables. No… that's not right." Shane's hands came out of his pockets when he felt that he had done something wrong. "Somebody's stealing," he mumbled in awe. "Somebody's… but who would be stealing?"

"Line up on the wall!" Bo ordered. "All of you! Let's go!"

Shane tried to calm himself from damn near having a panic attack. He knew that he couldn't have been wrong. He *hated* to be wrong.

"Shane," Apollo strong called him. "Come to your father, son."

He didn't hesitate to travel to Apollo's side to stand and wait for what the outcome could've been. After a minute, Apollo handed him something that looked like Tic-Tac's, and prompted him to chew them. Shane obliged and felt the wave of calm wash over him. They weren't Tic-Tac's. They were Valiums.

That day, someone had their throat slashed over trying to mess over Apollo's kid. Shane had no choice but to stand there and watch so that he would understand the dark side of the business. It wouldn't have been the last time either.

———————

Nine years living with Apollo and Shane saw the majority of the world. He witnessed the good side of up and everything in between. He was leaving the precinct after snagging Rich over speeding tickets and was ready to get into some weekend mischief when someone caught his eye. He stopped at his newly purchased Jaguar that he paid for with his own money. For so long he waited for Cherie to make her way back to Richmond, and he could've sworn that she was only a few yards away in a skirt suit, standing beside a BMW. She was thicker than a Snicker and favored Cherie. He had to do a double-take just to make sure that it wasn't her. In case it had been, he held his finger up to Rich, who kept shouting at him to get in the car, so they could leave already.

As soon as he took his first step toward the woman, the phone in his pocket vibrated. He clenched his jaw, hoping that it wasn't any of the sisters that he learned he had would be bothering him. Instead, it was his father.

"What's up, Pop?" he answered.

"You and Rich come to work," Apollo told him. "I have a very hefty job for you. These goddamn cockroaches need stomping," he informed him in code. By now, his son was more than capable of handling things on his own, whether it be about money, work, or taking out someone who thought they were competition.

"I got you."

Apollo hung up, and Shane pushed his phone back to his pocket, licked his lips, and prayed like hell that the young woman just wouldn't up and leave before he made it to her.

He approached the beauty, who was speaking on the phone with someone. Because of her jewelry, he could've sworn that she was a spoiled daddy's girl, and she was a diva. He gulped, pushed his hands into the pockets of his 501's, and politely waited for her to finish her conversation. He wasn't a pervert. He had his share of temporary women, but this one made him nervous. She looked so much like the one he lost long ago; he could've sworn that she was Cherie's sister if anything.

The young attorney hung up the phone and turned to Shane with a brow raised. He licked his lips and started to introduce himself before she cut him off. "De'Shane... *Hartford*, right?" she asked him.

He broke into a smile and tapped his thumb against his chin. "Maybe," he chuckled. "Who wants to know?"

"Nobody." She smirked and moved him aside so that she could get into her car. "I saw your photo ID in that one's file from you posting bail for him on four separate occasions. You keep that up and he'll never learn his lesson." She opened her door, slid in and reached out to close it.

Before she could, Shane grabbed the door and narrowed his eyes with a smirk on his face. "What's your name councilor?" he inquired.

"Jessica," she said with a smile. "Jessica Devaughn, Troublemaker."

"Ouch. She throws slugs."

"I do. You might want to get back to that $49,000 car of yours."

"49-5..." He smirked.

"You flirting with me, Mr. Hartford?"

A part of him didn't want to become involved, but it must've been fate when he was trying to let the memory of Cherie go. She was of legal age and could've returned to Richmond on her own if she was thinking of him. Here was a young woman who favored her so much with her own luxury car and an education. Maybe it was time to leave Cherie where she was. Maybe she just didn't want to come back. Maybe it was time for Shane to move on.

"Would I be too forward if I asked you to meet me somewhere tonight, Ms. Devaughn?"

Her smile grew. "And where would I be meeting you, Mr. Hartford?"

"The Roosevelt. It's intimate, quiet, and I hadn't eaten there in a very long time. I think you would like it."

"Seven," she said with a grin. "Don't be late, either."

He lightly nodded and closed her door for her. After throwing her a shy wave, he jogged back over to the Jaguar where Rich was up in arms.

"The fuck, Shane!" he yelled. "You gon' fuck my lawyer, huh? 'Cause if so, make sure you have her ass always down here so I don't have to call her uppity ass."

"Why you trippin'?" he laughed, as he started the car. "She's fine as fuck. It's just dinner."

"You ain't slick," Rich reprimanded him. "All this girl finna be is a surrogate Cherie, and you know it. First time I met her ass, that's the first thing I thought, but they ain't got the same hair or eye color. You know this is wrong, don't you?"

"I don't need a lecture," Shane said lowly with a straight face, and his eyes on the road. "I got to live, don't I?"

"Yea, but you got issues. If anybody knows, it's me. If it's anybody who's going to tell you without givin' a fuck about your temper, it's going to be me. And I'm tellin' you right now, right here, that you have a problem. You ain't lettin' Cherie go if you gettin' with somebody who could be her damn sister, bro."

"Rich, chill. I got this. I know what I'm doing."

Had he taken heed to his friend's warnings, he and Jessica would've been a match-made in heaven with as much as they had in common. However, Rich's words fell on deaf ears, and the entire relationship was plagued from the beginning.

Sometimes, you can salvage what's real...

CHAPTER ONE

Get On With It

Present day...

Standing at only five feet five inches with thick legs, wide and curvy hips, slim waistline and a bosom that you could probably bounce a quarter off of, Jessica truly named herself appropriately when she chose her stage name as Jessica Rabbit. The Black and Indian beauty had naturally long tresses that stopped in the middle of her back. Though her days of swinging from the pole were over, she still hung around the club during the nightshift to help girls with their makeup and hair, costume changes, and to kick in a little gossip. She had only been there for nearly a year after losing her license, but it wasn't hard to get to know your co-workers in a place like Safari's Gentlemen's Club.

The owner wouldn't let her onto the floor, so the bouncer had a plasma installed in the room so that the girls could see who took the main stage. It was fair to say that Jessica was pretty much liked by all she had come in contact with. All except for the Cruz sisters.

"Flawless!" a dancer screamed when she entered the room in nothing but her G-string and her boa covering her double-D implants. She had been referring to Jessica's red and shimmering eyeshadow. The Caucasian blew an air kiss at her colleague so that she wouldn't mess up Jessica's powdered red, full lips. The woman had gone over to the vanity to take out her diamond earrings, and found her next set of jewelry for her costume that Jessica had already taken out. "Such a fuckin' good one!" she exclaimed.

Suddenly, "Da Wop" by Lil Chuckee blasted from the TV's surround sound speakers and all of the heads in the dressing room had gone over to it.

A new girl that Jessica had just sent on her way was about to dance to her signature song. She had become a little teary eyed at the salute, because tonight was her last night at the club until her overprotective child's father would say that she could come back.

"That ass though!" the white woman screamed. "Jessie, you gonna let her outdo you?"

The others joined in when teasing her, and it pushed her to bust a move to show that she marked that song as her own for a reason.

She bent her knees and pulled her long and straight tresses up to make her ass jiggle and twitch to the beat of the song.

Even though she was being cheered on, the laughs and howls were silenced once the door opened and a man in all-black stepped through.

Jessica turned around to see him there with a blank expression on his face. Shane was dressed in all-black with the long sleeves of his shirt rolled up to the elbows. He looked like he had just clocked out for the day with the way he wore his dark tinted Ray Ban's at almost two o'clock in the morning, acid washed jeans and Nike boots that were slightly muddy.

Jessica rolled her eyes and found her purse inside her old locker, where the girls decorated the door of it with a thin blue sticker and a thin pink one to try and predict the sex of her baby.

LoreAnn, the white woman, gently grabbed her arm as she passed and whispered, "Girl, I wish I had that one. He looks like he'll have you strip at home, make it rain on you, and then fuck the shit out of you."

"You're so nasty," she giggled.

"Bye, Jessie!" the girls cheered one by one, some with saddened expressions.

She shyly waved at a few, and exchanged hugs with others before she could leave. Jessica was used to always wearing heels, but for the past three months she had no choice but to wear ballerina slippers. Her feet would randomly swell to the point where she could barely stand on them.

"Belly and ass!" the bouncer called as she passed.

Shane turned around and glared at him through his shades. The bouncer threw his hands up to surrender before he could get mauled in the parking lot.

Jessica turned around when she felt herself walking alone, backtracked and grabbed Shane by the arm to drag him to the car. "Seriously?" she asked him. "My kurta is over my butt, Shane. He can't even see it."

He spun her around to check her ethnic garment. It was ruby red with golden trims, and had wrapped around her neck. It stopped just below her womanhood, even though it stood up at the back some. He couldn't see her pregnant belly, even though she was so far along. Even Erykah had to admit that the girl had to be carrying the baby within her hips or her ass, because she didn't look over a day of the four-month mark.

"Still wearing tights though," he lowly complained as he pushed his shades up on the bridge of his nose. "Cover them thighs, girl." Playfully, he slapped her thigh, and she punched him in the arm.

"This is why you're single," she insulted him. "You don't know how to not be an asshole."

"And this is why I'm your baby's daddy because you love me."

Jessica opened her mouth to say something, but snapped her jaw shut. She wiggled her finger at him and said, "Touché, my brotha. Touché."

"Get in your car so we can go and get something to eat, please."

"Oh! Is that you being nice for a damn change?"

He flexed his jaw and tilted his head to the side. "Unlock the door so I can open it, Jessie. Stop playin'."

"Unlike any other chick that you've been dealing with, *De'Shane*, I can open my own doors and push my own whip. Thank you." She rolled her eyes as she moved his hand away from the handle of her BMW i8. She then lifted the butterfly door and slid in. "Don't you ever forget that I was Jessie before Shane."

"Knock off all them slugs, shawty," he warned.

"And this is how I know that you're not over her. I'll meet you back at your condo before I go to *mine*."

"It's like that?" he chuckled.

"What you thought? I was stayin' the night? Boy, please. You lured me in with food, and I came a calling because I didn't want you to throw a tantrum."

"Oh, you clownin' me tonight, huh?"

"Yezzer!" she joked, then let down the door of her car and cranked it.

Shane stroked his goatee as he backed away from her space to his Hummer.

One look at Jessica, and any man would ask why the hell he hadn't made things work with her. She had her own money, her own hustle, she was very intelligent, she was gorgeous, and could turn heads until necks snapped. But then any woman who had pushed up on Shane before, would remind those men that Jessica wasn't Cherie.

He smirked as he climbed into his SUV and unlocked the screen on his phone to check for his messages. These days, work never stopped. He needed to keep his mind clear before he sank into that darkness that he told Cherie about. It was a dangerous place to be, and without her, it would take him more than a while to come out of it.

"He went to Barnes and Nobel's today," the text read. *"He was with some woman at the spa around five, and it wasn't his fiancée."*

He responded to his message as "Work" by Rihanna flooded his vehicle, only it hadn't come from his speakers. He looked over to see the red glowing light from the BMW's undercarriage whisk past him. Knowing Jessica, she was probably wiggling in her seat to the song.

Life moved on, and he was desperately trying to do so again. However, he wasn't doing a very good job at it by having three goons and a private detective tail Terry wherever he went. One thing that should've never been mistaken about a quiet psycho like Shane was that he did stick to his word. When he made a promise, he followed through.

———

Jessica tossed her keys onto the coffee table and placed her purse and phone on the couch. Afterward, she traveled into the kitchen and grabbed a bottle of Jamaican Rum and two cans of Coke. When she sat them on the counter behind her, her cellphone blared from her purse. She hurried to it and saw that it was Ashington, Shane's little sister. She scrunched her brows at her screen, wondering why Ash wasn't asleep.

"You know better," she giggled when she answered. "Erykah is going to kill you."

"No, she won't," Ash grumbled. "Listen, I'm leaving this guy's dorm—"

"Ash, what the hell?" Jessica said with a hiss as she spun around. "You're already not supposed to be talking to me, but then you go to a guy's dorm?"

"Relax. He went to the bathroom. I wasn't comfortable staying. That's not why I called though."

"Well?"

"We took the DNA tests."

"Okay?"

"Jessie, things aren't right. You're going to have to represent someone when things come out. Alyssa had to retake hers because they found drugs in her system, and Jazz… well, she's scared out of her mind."

"What the hell?"

"It's all bad. I swear I've never been more afraid in my life."

"And that's only a manner of speaking because your little self is doing things that you have no business doing."

"True. But don't tell Shane I called, okay? He'll lose his mind."

"Your secret is safe with me. Text me when you make it home, alright? And don't do this again, Ash. It's dangerous. You're lucky that he hadn't drugged you or trapped you with his buddies."

"I know," she huffed. "I won't. I promise. And Jessie?"

"Yes?"

"No matter what my sisters say about you, I love you. Hopefully, my brother chooses correctly between either of you."

"Well, even though I'm slightly offended, I thank you. Lastly, your brother isn't choosing anyone. I'm just having his baby."

"And it's a good thing that he basically trapped you. I get to see you all the time, and I get a niece or nephew out of the deal."

"Goodnight, Ash," Jessica laughed.

"Night!"

She hung up and had gone back to the kitchen to have Shane's Coke and Rum ready before he ate. It was sad, but she knew everything about him and she wanted him to be comfortable.

When the lock turned to the condo, she had already put ice in his favorite Dallas Cowboys glass and had poured his drink.

"Barbeque!" she sang as she glided out of the kitchen with the glass in her hand.

"Nuh uh," he stopped her, closing the door with his foot. He then turned his face and leaned down to her.

"Asshole," she mumbled, then pecked his cheek. She then handed him the glass and took the bag from his hand.

"Thank you, baby."

"*Jessica*," she reminded him. "The name is Jessica."

"Oh, so I can't call you 'baby'?"

"Shane, you know what your problem is. You need to prove to me that I'm the only one for you, and then you have to take some anger management courses before you can even think about kissing these lips."

"So mean," he whispered, lifting the glass to his lips.

Jessica had taken the food into the kitchen to place everything on plates.

Shane made himself comfortable on his couch after pulling his shoes off and turning on the TV. Once she came back, she sat on the far end and tucked her feet underneath her with the plate on the arm of the couch. Shane looked down at his plate of ribs and potato salad, then over at her. A smirk slowly crawled across his face. He had to ask himself why he couldn't make something work with her, at least for the sake of his kid, but that same answer would creep back up on him. Every time it had, his facial expressions would fade and he would have to sip from his liquor, as he had done on this night.

"Put on *How to Catch a Predator*," Jessica said with a mouthful.

"Alexa," he called over his shoulder, to the little round black device that sat on the table near the front door of his condo. "*Play How to Catch a Predator.*"

"So lazy," Jessica teased. "The remote is right there in front of you. Right next to your plate, De'Shane."

"Aye, criticize me one more time."

"Don't get mad at me because you're lazy."

"I've had a long day—"

"Lazy, lazy, lazy… De… Shane… is… *lazy*."

Quickly, he swiped her legs from underneath her, snatched her plate and placed it close to his, and situated himself between her legs. "I dare you to say it again, girl."

She narrowed her eyes at him to where her lids were almost hiding the grey color to her orbs. She snarled and whispered, "Lazy."

Forcefully, he kissed her, and she didn't fight it. Instead, it took her breath away, and woke up everything in her that she thought she killed when moving on with her life. Shane had it. He had that way with her that she loved and hated at the same time. The only thing to stop her from begging him to take her to the master bedroom was

Cherie's name. Saying it to herself would always put out any fire. To Jessica, it was who he belonged to. As long as she reminded herself, she wouldn't get caught up into a nasty baby's mama and baby's daddy's girlfriend battle, if or when Cherie decided to pop up.

With minimal strength, she pushed him off, grabbed her purse and headed toward the door.

"You serious?" Shane questioned with a high-pitched voice. He followed her with his eyes, all the way out of the door.

Once inside of her car, Jessica let a tear fall while catching her breath. It was a painful feeling knowing that you dedicated yourself to someone, but they would never want you for who you are.

"I will never be Cherie," she mumbled to herself as she started her car. "I never will be, and he will never love me like I need to be. Bitch, you better remember that. You're just having his kid. That's all."

CHAPTER TWO

Hello, From The Other Side

*C*herie lounged poolside in her white bikini that she bought, knowing that Terry would lose his mind over her being in it. She didn't know what the big deal was with showing off her curves, but apparently, it would always send her fiancé flying up a tree.

Roxanna, a woman who used to be as curvaceous as Cherie but was now stout with no real appealing features. She had what most would call a "light-skinned mentality". Roxanna was the same shade as a graham cracker, yet she would debate with anyone who had perfect vision that she was high yellow and the same size as Cherie. She was also a submissive housewife who knew about the abuse that Terry brought upon the woman she claimed as a friend. Her only advise to Cherie was always the same. It was to love Terry and to keep him happy.

Cherie always thought that it was bullshit. How could she be a friend and not offer the slightest bit of her help?

"With all that happened back in Virginia, it was no wonder you came back to California," Roxanna said, lounging in a chair beside her.

Cherie found her exposed rolls in her two-piece to be repelling and repulsive, so she dared not to look over the rim of her white Ray Ban's at her because of her statement.

"You have a good man here, Cherie," Roxanna continued. "All you got to do is watch what you say. Especially if you want to snag that big ring."

"Is that how you got your husband?" Cherie asked dryly.

"I'm just saying. That Shane guy sounded like a complete nut job. He would've severely hurt you, had you stayed. You should count your blessings that you made it back home in one piece."

"Rox... can you hear yourself sometimes, when you speak? Shane wouldn't have physically hurt me. Terry, however—"

"Is your man."

So is Shane, Cherie thought.

"With your man, it's different."

Cherie tuned out the rest of what Roxanna was saying. She grabbed her phone off her bare stomach and unlocked her screen to check for messages and missed calls while her friend spoke. She only found three from the detectives who were listening over the tapes from the bugs that Cherie had placed in the house. They let her know that they were sending them off to the bureau to see if they had enough that would convict Terry of anything, or at least squeeze him enough to get a plea deal.

While scrolling, she found the message that she sent to Shane about not knowing how far along she had been, and her eyes welled.

He hadn't spoken a word to her since then. Even when he walked out of her home that she shared with Terry, he hadn't even looked at her. Could it have been that he stopped loving her? Did he stop caring? What about the chase? Cherie grabbed at her angle wing pendant on her necklace and thought about the promises that he made to her. How could he go back on all of them?

"Cherie?" Terry softly called her from the upper level behind the house.

He dressed down on today, wearing a plain white t-shirt and black and white plaid shorts. He brushed his waves and adjusted his rectangular framed glasses on his face, seemingly to make sure that he was put together for her. She knew better.

"Can I see you for a moment?"

She rolled her eyes and locked her screen back to go to his call. As soon as she was inside of the kitchen, Terry closed the doors and met her face with a backhand that sent her flying over to the island.

"What the fuck is wrong with you?" He roared. "Showing your fuckin' body off like that."

Cherie met his strength with a cutting board to the side of his face.

Terry's large body thudded against the floor, and the only thing he could do was to hold his ear and look up at the young woman he thought would never strike him back. With a trembling hand, he pulled it away from his ear and found crimson trickling between his fingers.

"You made my ear bleed," he said with shock in his voice.

"You ever fuckin' hit me again and I swear I will take that fuckin' hand off of you."

"You're fuckin' crazy."

"You're damn right I am. Now rethink the next time you want to raise your damn hand to me, Terry. Fuck wrong with you?"

Terry, shivering, watched her as she took the back set of stairs up to the second level.

Cherie galloped up the stairs and to the master's bathroom. She checked her lips for swelling and found none, then turned her bottom lip over, just to make sure that no skin had been broken. "Weak ass," she commented as she straightened her locks over her shoulders. "Still pretty, though."

After making sure that she was still put together, she went back into the kitchen and found Terry browsing through her phone. She wasn't at all worried, seeing as how every message that she received from the detectives were erased after being read. She cocked a brow and placed her hand on her hip.

"And what might you be seeking while going through my phone?" she asked.

"I'm trying to see where you got a sudden burst of confidence and strength," he responded, tossing her cell onto the island. "You ever hit me again—"

"Terry, shut the fuck up." Cherie rolled her eyes and reached for her phone.

Terry grabbed her wrist, and she yanked away from his grasp.

"You didn't learn your lesson yet?"

"You fucked him, didn't you?" Terry seethed. "His dick got you all Super Woman and shit?"

"His *dick* has nothing to do with it. I'm sick of you. To be honest with you, I don't even want to be here. You need me, *Terry.*"

"I don't need you, Cherie," he lightly chuckled.

"Shit," she giggled. "You do." Then, she yanked her phone off the island, scrolled through it and pulled up her recorder app to press record on it. Her intention was to get underneath his skin and get him to fess up so that she could leave.

Cherie hopped up on the island and placed her phone inside her bikini top.

"Ain't you supposed to be packin' or some shit?" He asked with an attitude.

"Tell me something," she perked. "Did you know that you were affiliated with the Chinese Mafia?"

"What?" His face scrunched as he took a step back.

"You have me in a situation that basically holds me prisoner here. So, I want to know. I need to know what the hell is going on, from point A to Z."

"Cherie, it's none of your business."

"That's bullshit. When you came to my aunt's funeral, you told me that my life was in danger. You told me about how I handled the accounts, and I didn't know what the fuck I was doing. You got me into this. Not only did you fuckin' beat me and tell me to mind my own business, but you dragged me into possibly gettin' my life taken away. You're honestly going to stand here and leave me in the dark?"

Terry ran his hand down his face instead of giving her an answer.

Cherie shrugged and hopped off the island and jetted up the stairs. It hadn't taken her long to grab her luggage out and start to toss clothes into it.

"Come on, " Terry said from the doorway. "You're leaving now?"

"I sure am," she said happily.

"Cherie..."

"No. You lied to me. That's what you did. You lied to me to keep me from Virginia because you know that there was someone there who couldn't live without me."

"No."

"You kept me away from my family, my friends—"

"The mafia will fuckin' kill me!" he blurted.

Cherie froze and had gotten wide eyed.

"To jumpstart the sports agency, they gave me a loan, alright? With that loan, I was able to bribe athletes into signing with me. After I paid that loan off, they came to me and told me that I owed interest. No matter how much I paid after that, it wasn't enough. To keep my damn life, I had to use accounts to transfer my so-called interest. Only recently I found out that the accounts I was sending money to had been those of athletes who were murdered. It was all connected and I didn't want a part in that. What the fuck else was I supposed to do when I knew that they knew who you were when going into the bank to put money into the business account? I was trying to save you from that. Being in Virginia is not where you need to be right now. It's safer here."

Again, she rolled her eyes. Cherie zipped up her luggage and pulled her phone out of her top. "You mean to tell me that you had no idea what was going on?"

"I was trapped, Cherie."

"And you didn't think to go to the police?"

"They *own* the fucking police!" he stressed.

"And it was never important for you to tell me until I had already left, to grieve the passing of my aunt?"

"You're missing my point. I've told you now. Now you have to stay."

"That's bullshit. How much am I involved, Terry?"

"They just know you. They knew that I kept you out of it, but they know that you're my fiancée, so they will try to use you as leverage."

Cherie turned off the recorder and sent it via email to the address she was already given. "Terry, I once thought that you could fill every single void that I had," she confessed. "I never knew my father, but I thought that you could replace that by loving me. You were so suave when we first met, and now... you're nothing. I thought you really loved me. That was another void I needed to fill. Let me tell you a quick story."

She pulled her luggage close to the door and sat on the edge of the bed to check for flights. "There was once this boy who was only twelve years old. He used to worship the ground I walked on, and for the life of me I couldn't understand why that was. He protected me, he fed me, and he did whatever it took just to make sure that I was okay. But then my mama drags me to New Mexico, South Carolina, and then to California. I never saw him again, but I saw much worse. He's a crazy fucker; he really is. I showed up for one event and was exposed to a hell of a lot more. Whereas everything I touch here is yours, as you put it… His crazy ass built something specifically for me. Every step, every piece of limestone, every karat of silver was mine. Not his, but mine. He walked through hell and back and waited for me, Terry." After clicking on a flight that was leaving in six hours, she looked up at him with seriousness in her eyes. "Now, in an hour, I'm walking out of that front door, and you're not going to stop me. Because if you try, it'll take one phone call to end you. Understand? And when I'm gone, you will not come after me, you won't know me, and you won't even speak to me."

"You're shittin' me, right?"

"Not by a long shot. Take care of yourself."

Cherie rose from the bed and had gotten into the shower to wash what little chlorine off of her that was there, and then twisted her locks into bantu knots so that she could take them down after they dried to have wild and spiraling curls. She dressed in a pair of fitting jeans and her favorite black leather booties, a tank top and a denim jacket. Afterward, she was on her way out of the door.

The only thing to stop her was faint moaning coming from the kitchen. A part of her wanted to lash out at Terry for banging someone who was supposed to be her friend, when said friend was married to his own, but she swallowed it and walked out of the door anyway.

"Karma's a bitch," she said proudly.

This time, she had taken Terry's favorite Jaguar. Since she had two hours before she needed to check in, she decided that she could go to her favorite bistro and get an omelet before leaving for good. Only, when she had gotten outside, Terry came marching up the sidewalk with flared nostrils.

"You're stealing my shit now?" he complained, waving his cellphone at her as he approached. "You mad, because your friend has better pussy than you?"

"You're so pathetic," she declared. She tried to pass him to get to his car, yet he grabbed her by the arm to pull her back. "We are in public," she spat. "Act like you have some manners."

He slung her against the wall of the bistro and closed the space between them. "You leave, and I will fuckin' hunt you down. You hear me, bitch?"

A man, seemingly appearing out of nowhere, whacked Terry in the back of the head. Then, another bomb rushed him from the side. Instead of asking questions, Cherie scurried to the Jaguar and took her leave.

Once she was parked at the airport, she happily keyed the Jag before locating her gate. She could feel her freedom and she wasn't going to jeopardize it by apologizing to him for anything.

"Mandy?" she called her cousin while sitting at her gate with her legs crossed. "Cousin, I'm coming home."

"Rie… umm… hey," Mandy stammered. "You're…? You're coming home… right now?"

"Yes," Cherie giggled. "I'm at my gate. My flight doesn't leave for another two hours."

"Cherie, I don't know how to tell you this… but umm… Well, you see, I never wanted to hurt you by telling you anything about Shane, which is why I never relayed messages between either of you."

"Cousin, spit it out."

"Shane—"

"Babe!" Rich called her. "We're going to be late! Let's go!"

"Late for what? What about Shane?" Cherie asked in a panic.

"Look, Rie," Mandy said somberly. "I'll just see you when you get here."

"Mandy?... Amanda?" Cherie pulled the phone away from her ear to look at her own wallpaper, and blinked back the panic that consumed her.

On a whim, she sent Shane a text message, asking him if he was okay.

Little did she know, he was driving, and Jessica saw the message on his notification bar.

She cut her eyes at him and asked, "Are you okay, De'Shane?"

"What?" he asked through a chuckle. "Why wouldn't I be?"

"*Cherie* wants to know." She pointed at his phone, mounted on the dash inside the holster. That name haunted her in her damn sleep. She didn't think, with the way Shane had been acting, that she would see it

30

anytime soon.

His smile faded, he gulped and flexed his jaw. Then, he snatched the phone off of the dash and turned it off.

"Don't be so dramatic," Jessica told him. "You could've answered her."

"I'm not going to disrespect you like that."

"We're not together, De'Shane."

"I really wish you would stop reminding me."

"And I wish you would face facts like I have."

"Jess, can we have one fuckin' moment of peace without you throwin' up in my face that I fucked up and we can't be together? Huh? Can we smile and be fuckin' merry like everything is jazzy, all for two whole fuckin' seconds?"

"Everything ain't ever goin' to be merry, because you decide to closet a lot of shit instead of talk about them. On top of that, you're the one who won't see life for what it is."

"Why should I? So, I can grieve the loss of a woman who actually reciprocated the love I had for her at one point? And then sulk over the loss of another woman who I basically praised? I ain't gonna do that."

"That's what you have to do to get through things."

"I've hurt enough. I'm not doing it."

"Look... after today... I just want out, alright? You can see your kid whenever you want, but—"

"What you mean, you want out?"

"I mean that this was the shit I didn't want to step back into."

"What shit, man? I don't even talk to that girl!"

"It doesn't matter, De'Shane! She's still going to hold that place in your heart, and you need to realize that you will never be able to erase her to give me the space that you say you want to give me."

"Jessie, fuck! What do you want from me?"

"You're not listening."

For her to make that statement, it struck him. Cherie told him the same thing. What was he not listening to?

"Let's just go to this lavish ass baby shower, that I specifically said that I didn't want, and get this shit over with," Jessica grumbled.

Shane was only lucky that she hadn't taken her own car. He only thought that her riding with him would make her see that he was willing to do what he did for Cherie, but for her and her only.

With her arms folded over her large bosom, Jessica peered out of the window. She was still battling the pain of knowing that she was someone's second option when they had been her first and only.

CHAPTER THREE

The Real Deal

*W*earing happy faces, Shane and Jessica cut the three-tier cake that poured out M&Ms from the center. Even though his sisters weren't too thrilled about him chasing after Jessica, they still slapped smiles on just for him. He had specifically asked them to be on their best behavior.

A man with olive colored eyes reached out to shake Shane's hand, and he took it into his own. When Josiah, Jessica's father, pulled him into a hug, he whispered, "Do what you have to do to make my baby girl happy."

"Yes, sir," Shane assured him.

Shane had gotten to a place where he wanted to be, and that was happiness. Maybe it hadn't been with the person that he wanted, but he was happy. He had told himself that chasing Cherie and putting so much into her was a mistake. He had to grow up, and he had to face facts that he was living in a fantasy when banking on his childhood love accepting him. It was a very hard pill to swallow, yet he had to with no water.

After the baby shower, they still hadn't done a gender reveal because neither of them wanted to know until it was time for the delivery. Shane had taken Jessica by the hand to the Hummer and loaded her in, then helped Rich to load the gifts in the back so that he could take her home. On the way, he had gotten a call from Apollo. He needed his son at his side, and he needed him now.

Shane helped Jessica into her apartment and had taken the gifts up to the living room. Then, he took it upon himself to fetch her a glass of ice and ginger ale.

Jessica made herself comfortable underneath her covers, and found the remote to her TV on her nightstand. As soon as she grabbed it, Shane was gently placing the glass down. She rolled her eyes and turned on the TV to see what was on at that time.

"Why you got to have an attitude, Jessie?" he lowly asked her as he took a seat on the side of her bed.

She smacked her teeth. "We're not in the public anymore, De'Shane. You can stop pretending that you give a shit."

He squinted at her and cocked his head to the side. "You for real right now?"

"Very much so."

"What's the problem? Huh? I'm trying, and you have this brick wall up that, every time I knock at it, you put up another fuckin' layer."

"You want to know what my problem is, Shane?"

He snatched the remote out of her hand and turned the TV off. "You're damn right, I want to know what the issue is."

"*You are* the issue!" she screamed.

"How? I ain't did shit, but show you attention and love."

"And it's fucking false!"

Shane dragged his hand down his face and almost scratched his eye with the golden ring on his pointer finger that had a handcrafted sun in the middle of it, which matched Erykah's.

"You keep doing all of this for what exactly? So, that can you just leave me and go back to Cherie whenever the fuck she shows her face?"

"Jessie, it ain't even like that," he mumbled.

"Oh, it ain't? And how the fuck is not? When we were together, all you did was compare me to her, Shane. You talked about more that you did with her than the shit you actually did with me! Then, your sisters had no problem rubbing it in my fuckin' face, every chance they got, just to remind me that there was someone out there who was supposedly better than me!"

"And I'm sorry for that—"

"Keep your apology! This is the prime reason that we can't be together. I'm not her, and I never will be. I've accepted it and you need to."

"If I wanted her, I would've chased her back to Cali. But I didn't," he snapped. "I'm here with you, trying to make shit work. So, what's the issue with trying to mend the past? Jessie, what the fuck do you want from me? You want me to step the fuck off?" He stood, and it made Jessica's heart drop.

She was confused. She didn't know if she wanted him to leave or stay, simply because she knew that what he was saying was true, but she was still battling with herself of if she should've stayed away and kept the baby to herself. Jessica was having serious trouble trying to separate what was fact from fiction. She knew that Shane would go to the ends for her like no one ever could, yet he might as well had been property of Cherie.

"Tell me, Jessica. Fuck!"

"I can't with you," she said no higher than a whisper.

"Fuck it." Shane whisked out of the room with his anger flaring and hurt stinging his heart.

Jessica, however, sat in her bed with her arms folded and a tear threatening to spill over. She didn't want him to go, but she didn't want him to stay either.

Shane jogged down to the Hummer, and pulled his phone out of his back pocket to call Apollo back.

"Go and check on Jazzie," Apollo told him. "Bo has to stay here with me, and I guess everybody else has their own agenda to where they can't pick up a fuckin' phone."

Shane started the SUV and frowned. It didn't sound like Jazz not to answer for their dad. "Consider me on my way, daddy."

"Call me when you get to her."

"I will." He hung up the phone and placed it on the dash. "What the fuck is going on?" he mumbled.

Upon arrival at the apartment complex, Shane noticed Erykah's car in the visitor's space and narrowed his eyes at it. If she was there, why hadn't she called anyone?

He got out and tugged at the end of his black and white plaid button up, and tread across the parking lot toward the building, then up the steps. He could hear Erykah begging for her sister to open the door.

"Rick, what's up?" he asked when he saw her.

Erykah turned around and showed him the mascara that was running down her face. Erykah was as tough as steel and rarely ever cried. She had to have been scared and hurt. "She won't answer," she sobbed. "Nobody has a fucking key, and I already called the police. They told me that she had to be missing for more than forty-eight hours before I could report her missing."

"Move back," he prompted her. He pulled his set of keys out of his pocket, found the key with the print of a queen of hearts card on it, and shoved it into the lock.

When Shane opened the door, the lights in the apartment were off and the brother and sister could feel the dread seeping out of the living area. Shane was almost afraid to flip the light switch near the door, seeing as how Erykah had barged in. He didn't know what they would see had he done so.

Sharply, Erykah turned to her brother on the balls of her heels and leaned her head over. He gulped and flipped the switch. What he saw made him want to pass out.

Erykah took heed to her brother's wide eyes and slowly turned around. Her shriek would never leave Shane's thoughts. As soon as she dropped to her knees, Shane scurried into the kitchen to grab a butcher's knife so that he could cut Jazz down from the light fixture she dangled from. Her once honey glow was a grayish color, and guilt consumed Shane when seeing it. He should've been thinking about her. Since leaving Augusta, everybody knew that Jazz wasn't okay, yet he was selfish, and only thought of his own situation. He had a duty to keep the family together in his father's absence, and he was failing. How the hell was he supposed to tell this to his father?

"Shane!" Erykah wailed as she pulled at the long t-shirt that Jazz was clad in. "Shane! Oh God! What did you do, Jazzie?" she sobbed, stroking her sister's face. "What did you do?"

"Rick, come on," Shane lowly said while cutting the last strand of rope from the chandelier. "You have to hold her so that she won't fall to the floor."

With as much strength as she had, she caught her sister's body and fell to the floor with her. Erykah couldn't feel the pain in her side. She held Jazz close, with her forehead pressed against her sister's as she cried.

Shane called the authorities and tried his best to get his words in order. Afterward, he pulled Erykah off the floor and squeezed her within his arms to try and calm her. They ended up on the floor, with him sitting and her between his legs. Her face was buried in the crook of his neck and her tears were soaking his shirt. His eyes were glued to Jazz. Her wild curls in particular. A few days from then, he wouldn't be able to see them any longer.

I should've been there, he thought. *Chasing the wrong shit and I let you down, Jazz. I'm sorry.*

Mandy and Rich stumbled through the door of the bungalow with grins on their faces. Those grins turned to small O's when they saw Cherie sitting on the couch with her legs crossed, enjoying whatever had been on the TV at the time.

"Hey, cousin," Mandy nervously sang, as she sloppily walked over to the couch to give Cherie a shy hug.

Cherie narrowed her eyes, then took them to Rich. "Godfather?" she asked him, noticing his black and white sash across his chest. "Who the hell was crazy enough to make you a godfather?"

"Um… baby, I think we left our plates in the car," Rich said, pointing over his shoulder.

"Hold up." Cherie stood on her bare feet and looked between the two as her mind raced. "Rich, you ain't got no damn car. How did y'all get here? Did Shane drop you?"

"Uuhh… no. Actually, I do have a car now, and uuhh…"

"Cherie!" Mandy perked with a smile as she dragged her cousin back down to the couch. "How was your flight? You still didn't tell me why you decided to come back home. The investigation over?"

"Might as well be," she answered, then turned back to Rich who was struggling to take his sash off. "Answer me, Richard. Who made you a godfather?"

He peered at Mandy, trying to telepathically receive permission to spill the beans on Shane being a father.

"Rich," Cherie called him through gritted teeth. "Who—"

"Shane!" he blurted.

Mandy ran her hand down her face over his mistake.

Cherie's neck bucked back as she counted on her fingers of how long she had been gone. "He's a father after three fucking months?" she complained. "And Amanda didn't tell me?"

"It's not like that, cousin," she defended herself. "It was news to me when we got the invitation, and I didn't want to hurt you by telling you."

"Oh, really?"

"Really. And I will not take the blame for whatever it is that you're feeling right now, when I thought I was being helpful and sparing feelings. Why don't you just leave and come back and get mad at something else, huh? This is the second time that I stand trial by minding Amanda's business."

"Babe, okay," Rich sympathetically said.

"No! Fuck that! First Shane comes down hard on me when she was the one who didn't come back because of other obligations, and now she wants to come in and try to sound like a skeptic over me trying to spare her. Whatever. I'm not the one who fucked somebody when y'all weren't together. Go to Shane about it. I'm out of this." Mandy stormed off to her mother's old room that she long converted into her own, and slammed the door behind her.

"You know, Cherie... life still moves on, even when you're not around," Rich mumbled.

"And what does that mean?" She worked her neck at him.

"It means that you chose to leave, and before then, you chose to stay away. This baby is in the middle and was only here because my boy tried to erase you because you never came back. By the way, Jessica is seven months. You do the math. He hadn't heard from you, and he gave up hope when he tried to make shit work with her. But then, you would have to think about her too. They couldn't work because she wasn't you. You poisoned him somehow."

"*Poisoned?*" she sneered.

"Yea, Cherie. Poisoned. Excuse me. I have to check on my woman. It seems as if she's damned if she does and damned if she doesn't. But from now on, keep her out of you and Shane's business. It ain't either one of y'all that got to pick her up after y'all dropped her. It's me." After his decree, he took his leave to make sure that Mandy was okay.

Cherie folded her arms and tightened her lips. Inside, she was cracking. He was having a baby on her and he should've known how much she loved him. However, she never stopped to express that love for him, yet he had on many occasions.

How dare he? She was supposed to have the first pick. She was supposed to have her happily ever after. Cherie felt that she was entitled to feel betrayed and hurt. One thing was for certain though. She and Shane needed to have a serious heart to heart after she popped him in the face for not even telling her himself that he was going to be a father.

———

Cherie caught an Uber to Shane's home, and used her remote to get inside the garage. After remembering that she needed a thumbprint to get into the house, she got her Tesla and returned to Mandy's. Rich was frantically backing out of the driveway when she returned, and it made her wonder what the hell was going on. She threw her car in park and pulled her phone out of her purse to send Shane a text, giving him a piece of her mind. Before she pressed send, she erased it and called him. She tried him three times to receive no answer. Knowing that the number four was his lucky number, she tried him one last time, but the person to answer was no him.

"Hello," Ashington answered with a sniffle.

"Ash?" Cherie quizzed.

"Yes?"

"Hey… where's your brother? Are you okay?"

"No. We have a family situation going on, and I really need to get back. I'll tell Shane you called."

"Wait! Is he okay? Is it your dad?"

"No. It's Jazz," she whimpered. "I got to go."

"Give me that!" someone shouted in the background.

"What happened—" Cherie pulled the phone away from her ear and looked at her phone to see that she had been hung up on. What the hell was really going on?

―――――――――

"We're not going to sit around and blame ourselves," Quita said with a folded piece of paper in her hand. She had read the short and simple note that Jazz left for her father and siblings, and no one sitting around Apollo's sitting room was upbeat.

Shane sat in the corner in a tall back chair with his elbows propped up on his knees and his fingers clasped together into his fist underneath his chin. Erykah couldn't keep her eyes off of her brother. She knew that he wasn't made of stone, yet he tried to be for the sake of the family. She was waiting for a tear to fall from his red eyes. The vein that grew from the hook of his nose and exploded between his eyebrows exposed his flaw. He was fighting back tears purposely.

"Brother," Ashington sweetly called him as she approached, and stopped in front of the lit fireplace to sit on her knees, facing him. "It's going to be okay, alright?"

He didn't return a statement.

A squishing sound and the soft hum of a motor could be heard in the distance. Apollo was rolling down the hallway on the marble floor in his wheelchair. His condition was worsening, and he couldn't do anything on his own. The nurse that was assigned to him, tried to keep up with him beside his electric chair. He was on a mission to place his children at ease.

Upon entering his sitting room, the first person that he saw and made contact with was Leelah, Jazz's mother. The corner of his top lip quivered. "Fuck are you doing here?" He seethed.

The woman who looked like she could be his child as well, crossed her long and skinny legs as she pushed her back into the plush sofa next to Erykah. With the way,   she was dressed in a black silk nightgown and tights, anyone could tell that the money that was being given to Jazz was handed over to her.

"My child just did the unthinkable," Leelah sneered.

"*My* child," he said with a hiss.

43

"Since when, Apollo? You didn't know shit about her until Joyce came knocking—"

"Whoa, nuh uh! Keep my name out of it," Joyce defended herself. "You want to scold him, then that's fine. But don't you put me in anything. I was doing what was right for the kids."

"You know what? You can shut the fuck up! You always got to be Miss Perfect, don't you?"

"Hold the fuck on," Erykah said lowly. She was snatching out her earrings on cue to tag Leelah for raising her voice at her mother.

Ashington jumped off the floor and about-faced to sit in her sister's lap to keep her from getting up.

"Bitch, you better watch the fucking way you talk to that one!" Erykah shouted. "You ain't the motherfuckin' factor, alright? We just lost our sister! Now what my daddy asked you needs to be answered, instead of you jaw jackin' and shit! Answer the fuckin' question, Leelah!"

"Better yet, tell us how long our sister was battling bipolar depression," Quita said, flailing the note in her hand.

"I can answer that," a quiver surfaced.

All heads, except for Shane's, turned to the entryway of the sitting room. The glow of the fireplace cast upon Alyssa's skinny body, and the first thing that everybody noticed was that she had put on some weight in the last three and a half months. Her skin was clear and she was wearing her natural hair. Even though she was clad in simply a white t-shirt and boyfriend sweats, she still strolled into her father's sitting room and stopped in front of Leelah.

"What?" Leelah asked, working her neck at Alyssa.

Out of the blue, Alyssa backhanded Leelah and hardened her face. "You knew longer than I did, bitch," she said through closed teeth. "I called my sister to have her sing to me, because I was having a moment and thought that I was going to go crawling to the needle. She told me that she didn't have it in her."

"What does that have to do with me?" Leelah shouted.

"She told me that you told her not to take her medication because the government was going to help her better than the medication."

"No, I—"

"Lie on my sister and I will fuck you up where you sit."

"Alyssa, she ain't worth it," Quita said.

"Oh, she's worth it. My sister told me that she was empty inside." Her voice croaked at the end of her sentence. "That was two fucking days ago, you bitch. And as far as Mama J being Miss Perfect… she might as well be, because none of you other bitches were ever real mothers to us. Why? Is it because you couldn't have Apollo all to yourselves? Because you had to share him with so many different kids? Well let me tell you something. I ain't on drugs now. Been damn clean for three and a half months, and I see shit a lot clearer. Just like I can see that your ass got my sister's blood on your hands. Get out of my daddy's house."

"Who are you to—"

"I said get your motherfuckin' ass out of my daddy's house before I snatch Ash off Erykah!" She pointed past Quita to prompt Leelah where she could go.

In turn, Leelah rolled her eyes and left the house without so much as a fight to stay. She knew what she had done wrong, and there was no use in debating it.

Then, Alyssa turned to Shane in the corner and saw how still his face was; how solid he sat in the corner. She went to him and pulled him up by his hand, and wrapped arms around his neck. "I'm sorry, brother," she whispered. "We all have suffered losses every now and again. It's a way of life."

Shane's body was vibrating within Alyssa's arms and he almost broke. He couldn't stand the thought of losing again, and the guilt of not being there for Jazz weighed heavy on him.

"Shane, stand up," Apollo told him strongly from across the room. "We all will get through this. Together. As a family."

Joyce reached down and touched his hand, then squeezed it as hard as she could to give him comfort. He looked up at her with confusion in his eyes and felt a tingling sensation in his hand that he hadn't felt in years. His woman was right beside him, where she belonged years ago.

Rich came to retrieve Shane in his time of need and took him back to his condo. After seeing to it that his friend was okay, he left him to his thoughts. Shane laid in his bed and pulled his phone out of his pocket to place it on the charger pad. His body was so heavy that he didn't dare to even take his shoes or clothes off.

Ashington was reluctant to stick by her brother's side. Going back to her dorm was out of the question, and going home to her mother was not an option. At least with Shane, she knew that she wouldn't have to deal with him whimpering and crying, and if anything, they could console each other if need be. Even Alyssa tagged along, just to make sure that he was going to hold up. It was the least she could've done after all of the trouble she caused.

The two claimed the second bedroom of the apartment and borrowed a few of his shirts to sleep in, taking turns to keep an ear out for him in case he flew off into a rage.

A knock came at the front door and the sisters sat up in the king-sized bed, alert. Alyssa made Ash stay, and grabbed her brother's spare gun from underneath his recliner before answering the door.

On the other side was Jessica, dressed in her tights and a long t-shirt. She let herself in and dangled her key up at Alyssa. "Sorry," she apologized. "I couldn't find my key. I was panicking."

"What are you doing here, Jessica?" Alyssa questioned. "I thought y'all broke up."

"We did. I'll explain later. Shane texted me. Where is he?"

"He's in the room."

She ripped away from the living room, and rushed into bedroom where she found Shane laying in his bed, staring up at the ceiling.

"Baby, are you okay?" she worried. Jessica threw her purse onto the dresser, and quickly waddled over to the bed.

Shane had done something that he never did with her, nor had he noticed that she called him something other than his name. He rolled over and laid his head in her lap, and let out silent tears.

Jessica stroked his dreads and let him cry out all of the hurt in his body until he fell asleep. Then, she moved them both over and coached him into getting underneath the covers. He wrapped his arm around her waist and pulled her close. She didn't oppose either. Jessica fit the groove of his body and relaxed a little. Even she didn't realize that she had fallen into old habits, and she was so far gone that she couldn't even get up and stick to her guns.

"I'm so tired of losing," Shane grumbled into her hair.

She lovingly stroked the hand that he rested against her belly instead of giving him a response.

"It's okay," he grumbled with a sniffle. "I'm gaining one. Who's ever in the oven will never know what losing feels like. I can bet you that. This baby will be nothing but happy, at all cost."

"Shane…"

"I don't want to lose anymore, Jessie. I'm not ever going to again."

She sucked in a slow and shaky breath before lowly declaring, "You won't have to."

CHAPTER FOUR

You Had To

*T*hree days of gloom hanging over everyone wasn't easy. The feeling of being unwelcomed most definitely ate at Cherie. She decided that getting a suite at a hotel while she hunted for jobs and apartments would be a better fit for her. She couldn't stomach her cousin's sudden burst of anger. Mandy and Rush were looking at her like she was the bad guy, when Mandy knew why she had to go back home. Where was she to stand up for her instead of ridiculing her?

To get all of the stupidity off her mind, Cherie decided that she needed a little retail therapy. Besides, it wouldn't hurt to stock up on her wardrobe since she didn't bring much with her from California.

Purposely, she drove her Tesla, calculating how long it would take Shane to realize that it was gone. Two hours into spending Terry's money this time, she stepped out of Banana Republic with only two bags in her hand. She had already raided Victoria's Secret and H&M, and had put the bags in the car. Now, she wanted to go into Footlocker for a few pair of kicks for when she wanted to dress down.

The sight she stumbled upon was one that made her blood

simmer and sizzle.

————————

2 hours prior…

Jessica had placed the last platter onto Shane's small dining room table, and ran her fingers through Ashington's hair, who was sitting at the table already stuffing her face. Alyssa caught her arm before she could pass and threw her a smile. She returned it and swayed into Shane's room to crawl on top of him.

He looked so at peace while he was sleeping and she couldn't resist him any longer. There was no use in fighting what she knew was there. She leaned down and gently kissed his lips to wake him. Then, she ever so slowly stroked his sideburns.

"You need a lineup," she said no higher than a whisper. "Get up, De'Shane. You have things to do."

"No," he grumbled as he smoothed his hands up her thighs, hips and waist. "Why can't we just stay here?"

"Because money doesn't sleep, and you need a shower. It's been two days. You need to get up, don't ask questions and let Jessie handle the rest."

"What I get for it?"

She bit her bottom lip at feeling his hands softly squeezing her cakes through her tights. "You'll see after you get up." Playfully she slapped his face and gave him a genuine smile that he hadn't seen in a very long time.

Shane gripped the back of her thighs, and rose from the bed with her. Without paying attention to her giggles, he waddled with her inside of the master bath, and placed her on her feet.

"What are you doing?" she whined. Her hands were pressing into his chest, yet it hadn't stopped him from turning her around. "Shane... come on."

"You come on," he grumbled as he pulled her tights down a little.

"Shane, we can't."

"I don't see you stopping me." With his fingers, he wiggled them between her slit and felt a puddle splash onto his tips. "I see you want this."

"We can't do this," she whined again. Jessica gripped on to the sink with her head bowed and her chest heaving.

It wouldn't be long before she felt his manhood at her opening.

"God!" she gasped at his insertion.

"Fuck," he grunted.

"Shane, think about this. We might get our feelings involved—"

"You're the only one fighting those feelings."

Harder he pushed into her, and he forced her to put a natural arch in her back. She was too deep in just to back out now. Those old habits would cost her indefinitely.

"Damn, Jessie," Shane moaned.

She was damn near biting off her bottom lip to keep her sounds inside. She dug deep and found the strength to move away from him. Jessica pushed her palms into her eyes until she remembered that her tights were pulled down. She pulled them up and fingered her locks to the back. "Look, you just lost your sister, okay?" she spoke with sense. "This isn't the right move to make. You're vulnerable, and you're not thinking clearly."

"Why you keep fightin' me, Jessie? Damn."

"Just… just get in the shower and we can talk about this another time. Not right now. I'm on a mission, and I plan to succeed."

"Jess—"

"You. Shower. *Now.*"

He rolled his eyes and dropped his boxer briefs to climb into the shower as instructed. Whatever she had planned had better been worth it.

Jessica took the time to go to her own home, only fifteen minutes away, and showered and changed clothes. When she returned, she expected Shane to be trimming his goatee. Who she ran into, however, was Erykah. She was getting out of her car when Erykah was stepping out of her own.

Erykah rolled her eyes at Jessica and chirped the alarm to her car. "Not surprised to see you slithering around here," she said with attitude.

"And why am I not surprised that you're angry at the world?" Jessica shot back.

"Look, *Princess*, my brother has a lot on his plate—"

"And I'm not here to make it worse, alright? I'm planning on taking him out on the town and breathe a little life into him."

"Yea, right."

"You know that you're the only one besides Quita who doesn't like me? Alyssa and Ash are up at the apartment now. I made them breakfast. You know what? You're welcome to some if you want. You see, I'm not as hateful as you. Shane and I aren't together. Even though you made me lose my license, I don't hold any hate against you because you didn't put a gun to my head to make me fight back to make myself look bad. However, you continue to make yourself look bad very often."

"Excuse me?"

"There's no reason for you to constantly be a bitch, Erykah, yet you choose to do so. Do me a favor by keeping all of that negativity away from Shane. I have to spend the day building him up. Something that none of you decided to do."

"Bitch, I should pop your ass in the mouth for that."

"Yea, and you would be proving my point of how much of a bitch you are. You should work on that." She gave Erykah a wink, then jogged up the stairs to check on Shane.

As soon as Erykah entered, she exchanged hugs with Ashington, and eyeballed Alyssa. "Why you ain't tell nobody that you were getting clean, girl?"

"Why do you have to be such a bitch?" Alyssa shot back as she rolled her eyes. "Besides, you couldn't give two shits about me. The least I could do is make my daddy proud before he leaves us all for good."

Jessica couldn't stay to listen to the sisters' quarrelling. She re-entered the master's room and found Shane putting on his Ralph

Lauren boots on the side of the bed. She animatedly clapped her hands at seeing that he had taken the time to have one of his sisters braid his dreads into two long braids over his shoulders.

"What you so happy for?" He grumbled as he stood.

"You're up and moving around."

He snatched her by the hand and pulled her into a hug.

When she gasped, she inhaled his scent and felt tingly all over. "God, and aren't you smelling delicious."

"Let's go and get this over with."

"Shane—"

"Let's go, Jessica."

She placed her hands on her hips while he left the room, tilting her head. He just wasn't going to let up until he had gotten his way.

Shane kissed both Alyssa and Ash's cheeks before heading to the door. He looked over at Erykah on his couch and smirked. "Fix that face, Rick," he said.

"You fix yours," she snapped. "Why is she here? It was bad enough that we had to play nice at that damn baby shower."

"*I'm* here because Shane needed me," Jessica spoke up for herself as she fixed the straps to her purse at her wrist. "Instead of fixing your face, you should fix your attitude because Miss Jessie ain't here for all of that. I'm here for *him*."

"You gon' let her talk to your sister like that, Shane?"

"Man, I ain't here for that shit either." He snatched the door open, and left the apartment. "Be nice," he called over his shoulder. "And don't fuck up my shit while I'm gone!"

Jessica threw on her champagne tinted aviator styled shades and flipped her long curls over her shoulder. Erykah could kiss her backside for all she cared.

Finally, she caught up to Shane at his Hummer and shook her head at him. "And what do you think you're doing?" she asked him with her hand on her hip.

"Takin' the truck," he responded. "What it look like?"

"No. No, sir. We're taking my i8." She fished her keys from her purse and tossed them to him. "*You're* driving."

"Jessica—"

"Get in the damn car, De'Shane! And don't forget to open my door."

He shook his head and unlocked the doors with the remote in his hand, then waited for her to slide in. Afterward, he let the door down and went over to the other side to get in himself. "What are we doing?" he asked miserably before starting the car.

"We're going by the barbershop because you need a lineup, like I said. And then we're going to the mall—"

"I mean… *this*. Between me and you. What are we doing?"

"Look, you said you needed me, so I'm here, okay? Let's go and clear your head. I have a job to do for you, and you're hindering that."

"Whatever," he mumbled, and finally started the car to leave.

Jessica kept to her promise, even though she had to argue with Shane at the barbershop to let her pay for his lineup. Then, she had gone with him to the spa where they received hour and a half massages and manicures. Afterward, they enjoyed the sauna and talked about things that they had before. She learned a little more about Shane in the forty-five minutes that they sat there, like why his sisters were so overprotective, and why he truly thought that Cherie would be the one for him. He confessed again about how he should've stopped living in his head a long time ago, followed by an apology. Somehow, this time, Jessica accepted it, and gave him yet another genuine smile.

Feeling more relaxed and having a weight to be lifted off his shoulders, Jessica held his hand as he drove, and listened to him blame himself over Jazz's suicide. She had told him that it couldn't have been his fault because no one saw it coming, and that Jazz didn't open up enough to tell anyone about it. He was at ease a bit with her answer, even though he still thought that he should've been focused on the family instead of Cherie. Jessica decided to not even touch the subject of Cherie and kissed his cheek when he found a parking space at Chesterfield Towne Center. She could've sworn that Shane blushed when he put the car in park, and it made her smile.

Being a gentleman, he had gotten out and opened her door for her, then grabbed her hand to escort her into the mall.

"Now, we have to find you some sneaks," she said. "Don't fight with me over this, De'Shane. You're always doing everything for everyone else, so now it's time for someone to do something for you."

"Jessie—"

She stopped in between two shops and stomped her foot. "Do you want this or not?"

"Do I want what?"

"*Us*. Because if you do, then you have to remember that I don't always need Shane to come to my rescue, and that I will always be there for him, whether he likes it or not."

"Jessie—"

"Fine." She rolled her eyes and walked away.

Shane caught her waist and pulled her back a little. He walked with her in the direction of Footlocker with his lips gently against her earlobe. His hands slithered up her hips and underneath her long designer droop-neck blouse to grab onto her waist. "You know better than to just walk away from me, girl," he grumbled.

Shane always knew how to give Jessica goosebumps and it worked. Her nude colored lips stretched into a smile. A real one. Just like old times, he could put a smile on her face, even when being rude. Getting back into the groove wouldn't be so bad.

She sat him down on a bench close to the door and grabbed the first pair of Nike's she saw on the wall. "Look, babe. These are nice," she marveled. "You'll look good in these." She then handed him the black and white Metcon 3, hoping that he would like it.

He examined the shoe and smirked. "I think I would too," he lightly chuckled.

Jessica looked around the store for a cashier and spotted one near the register. "Excuse me!" she called with a smile. "Can we get the black and white Metcon 3's in a size twelve?"

Shane gently wrapped his hand around her thigh and pulled her closer to him. He kissed the stomach of her blouse and said, "Your mama's tryna get your daddy right, in here. What you think? Should I go with the Metcons?"

"Shut up," she giggled. "My baby's gonna have style, just like her mother."

He stood and towered over her, only to bend his neck and graze his lips over hers. "*Our* baby," he lowly reminded her.

From a few yards away, Cherie stood baffled at the sight of her Shane kissing another woman. And passionately, at that. Her stomach churned and her insides were on fire. She stood there and battled with herself over if she should've stomped into Footlocker to part them and tell Shane about himself, or if she should've just walked away. She stood there for a few more seconds and watched Shane try on a shoe, as Jessica kept her smile on her face. She remembered when Shane could make her smile like that. How could he have given that to someone else?

Instead of making a scene, she scurried to the Tesla and slammed the door after throwing her bags into the backseat. Angrily, she located her phone and let her anger take her on to a distant place where she thought she would never be. She phoned Shane and waited impatiently for him to answer. When receiving the voicemail, she was fuming.

"You are one piece of shit, De'Shane!" she yelled. "I can't believe I thought that all that shit you said and done was for me! You're a fucking liar and a cheat! You're a *liar*! I saw you today with that bitch who looks like a goddamn stripper! And here I am, thinking that you had more class than that! You have a baby with this bitch? A *whole* fucking baby?

And you couldn't be man enough to tell me that? This is why you don't return calls. Because you're with that fat bitch! Oh, but you sure as shit lived for me, huh? Fuck you, Shane! Fuck *you*! Fuck you, fuck you, fuck you, *Shane!*"

Still riding on adrenaline, Cherie threw her phone onto the floor and pulled out of her space with cloudy eyes. When in traffic, she could barely see, and with a heavy heart, it was hard to make good decisions. She ended up swerving to get from behind a slow driver, when actually they were doing the speed limit. That would be something that would get her into much trouble.

She wiped her eyes with the back of her hand, then swerved from the middle lane, over onto the far right. However, she hadn't seen the city bus that was on the side of the 18-wheeler. To avoid it, she swerved to the right again and off the road, where she slammed into a tree.

CHAPTER FIVE

True Colors

With Jessica resting on his arm later that night, Shane fell asleep with the weight of the world off his shoulders. His cellphone kept ringing. He thought it had all been in his dream, yet it wasn't. With his free hand, he reached over onto his nightstand and pulled it off the charging pad. The unregistered number on his screen was blurry, so he answered anyway.

"Hello?" he answered groggily.

"De'Shane Hartford, please," a woman said on the other end.

"This is he."

"Hello, this is a courtesy call from State Farm. We received a notification in our systems that indicate that your Tesla 3 was pulled from the park near Chesterfield Town Center earlier by first responders, yet the accident was not reported by you, sir. It was registered at a wrecker's yard, instead. Is everything okay?"

"My what?" he asked hoarsely as he raised from the bed.

"Your Tesla 3, sir. License plate number BTB0764."

Shane swung his feet over the edge of the bed and thought about it for a second. That was his car, but how the fuck was it wrecked when…

"Shit!" he cursed aloud as he jumped out of the bed and scurried over to his closet. "Where is my car now?"

"Yes, sir. I can provide that information. Let me know when you're ready."

Shane listened to the woman blab about where he could find the car he bought for Cherie. Then, after throwing a shirt over his head, he called Rich and had him to start calling hospitals to see where Cherie could've been. She had a hell of a lot of explaining to do. Lucky for him, Jessica was knocked out cold. She hadn't heard a thing.

On the way out, he finally decided to check his missed calls, texts and voice messages. When he heard Cherie's angry voice, he just knew that she wrecked the car on purpose.

Rich hadn't taken long to meet him in the parking lot to rush up to the room. Shane pulled the hood from his black hooded shirt over his head and marched up to the elevator. With as many questions that roamed through his head, the only one that he was actually stuck on was how come she hadn't called him earlier, long before she saw him with Jessica? Why hadn't she just shown her face or something? Even if she was close, how come she didn't approach them and say something? It was funny how she could get mad because he was with Jessica, but she couldn't open her mouth to tell him that she was coming back to Virginia. The last he had heard of her was that Terry was about to hit her in public, and the goons he hired had stopped him from doing so, and stomped a mudhole in his ass for it. When the hell did she leave, exactly?

"They said she was in room 717," Rich told him as they stepped off the elevator and headed in the direction of the room.

"Cherie better not be unconscious when I get into this motherfucker," Shane said through closed teeth.

"Don't come in here," she complained, before he could even turn the corner.

When Rich and Shane laid eyes on her, she was sitting on the side of her bed in what she had on for that day— skinny jeans and a long blouse that had a drooping neckline. The only thing that was visually upsetting about the young enchantress was that she had a gash on her forehead, covered up by large gauze and medical tape. She scowled at the two who trampled into her room and made it known that she didn't want to see either of them.

"You wrecked the car and couldn't call me, Cherie?" Shane challenged her as he shut the door and locked it.

"Don't you start on who was or wasn't calling who, De'Shane. I called and you didn't answer. The last time I called your phone, Ash answered to let me know that something was going on, but she didn't tell me what that was. Quita snatched the phone from her and hung it up. I've been texting you too, but you never returned my messages. Oh, but I damn sure did see you with your baby mama at the mall. And when were you planning on telling me that you were going to be a father, De'Shane?"

"I didn't know about my kid until after you had already left. Don't work your little ass neck at me when you chose to leave and didn't hit me up for months. You made a decision—"

"To clear my damn name, and that's exactly what I did!"

"You decided to ex me out of your life, altogether, before you left. Don't pretend that we didn't argue before you left."

"I am not pretending about anything. I don't even want you here. How about you leave? Tell me how much the damages are going to cost and I'll make sure to pay for them."

"You know you ain't ever got to worry about that when it comes to me. I guess you got your niggas mixed up."

"Naw, you got your bitches mixed up to think that you can talk to me any kind of way. Why are you here, anyway? Shouldn't you be with her? Are you here to check on the car or me?"

"I'm not gonna do this with you. You push and pull me, and I'm done with it. To be honest with you, if I wasn't having a kid, I would've left here so I wouldn't have to suffer remembering your ass."

"Excuse me?"

"You heard what the fuck I said. I don't even want to go to my own house because of you."

"And that's my fault?"

"Because I built it for *you*!"

"You know what? I don't care what you supposedly did for me because it's all bullshit. If you didn't think that I really loved you, then you could've just stepped the hell off. It was you who kept pushing, and pushing—"

"And didn't get nothing in return. Tell it like it is. We were living in a damn fantasy. Not no more. That's why you saw me with my girl. I wish I would've stopped loving you a long damn time ago because you made me a fool for you."

"That's how you feel?"

"And to think... I still kept an eye on you when you went back to Cali."

"What?" she asked breathlessly.

"Your boy got his lights knocked out when he tried to put his hands on you in front of that restaurant, didn't he? Nothing in you said that you should try to figure out why?"

"That was you?"

"You damn right it was. Thought I was protecting you. But to move on and live life... *truly* live life... I got to let you go."

"You act like—"

"You're free, Cherie. I'll pay for my car. Do what the fuck you want to do." Shane backed away from the bed and whirled around to the door as she called his name repeatedly. He was so upset that he started to punch a wall before he could get to the elevator, yet he only flexed his fist and kept it moving like the adult he was striving to be. "I got to let her ass go," he mumbled.

Once they reached the cars, Rich looked over the hood of the Hummer and surveyed his friend for a moment. He knew that Shane had just severely hurt himself, yet he didn't know what to say. All that he could rustle was, "Are you sure that this is the right thing to do?"

"She doesn't love me, Rich," Shane said. "Ain't no way in fuck she could have. If I could move heaven and goddamn earth for that woman, then you tell me what I should've gotten back. Then, you can ask me what it was that I had gotten in return."

Rich dug into the pocket of his jacket and retrieved a rolled up Dutch Master, smelled it, and handed it to his friend. "Might as well get throwed before you go back to Jessica Rabbit."

———————

A week had gone by since Cherie had heard those hurtful words from Shane, but she tried her best to swallow it. She was only happy that after he said what he needed to, he was gone within a flash, or else he would've seen her tears fall. Nothing hurt worse than those words that he spewed to her, exactly seven days prior. Not even when she was forced to get out of Rich's car and hobble up to the porch of the bungalow. Thank God that she had clothes and toiletries there, or else she would've had to spend the remainder of the ride from the hospital wincing in pain at the many bumps in the road. She had sent Rich to the hotel to gather her belongings, and called the front desk to let them know that she was closing her account for a few days.

Upon arrival to the house, Rich received a text telling Cherie to check the mailbox. He was serious about moving on and trying to erase her, and to prove it, he placed his bracelet inside of an envelope with a sticky note inside it. The note read, *"Here's your halo back. Take care."* Cherie was furious. What had transpired for him to want to break her so badly? Either they seriously had their wires crossed, or the both of them had to grow up. That note and bracelet had Cherie in a bad mood for days to come.

Now, she sat on the couch with her foot propped up on a pillow on the coffee table. Even though Shane and Rich saw her sitting on the side of the bed, they missed the part about her planning to escape the hospital before her discharge. It wasn't like she was going to get far with a fractured shin. She didn't have anywhere to go or anything to do until her shin healed, which, according the doctor, was going to take her up to six weeks before she would even begin to remotely walk without a limp.

She folded her arms when she smelled the scent of Viva La Juicy in the air, taking the hint that Mandy was about to hit the door with Rich. Nobody had been paying her any mind as she sulked in her own feelings. As Rich, had said prior to this day, life moved on.

"Hey, boo!" Mandy cheered on the phone from the bathroom in the hall. Cherie could hear her loud and clear with the door open. "Oh, no, it's not a problem. I can't wait. Did you need me to do something specific, or…? Oh, okay. Well, I'll see you in a second, doll."

"Whatever," Cherie mumbled.

Shortly after, a knock came at the door and all she could do was look at it. She damn sure couldn't get up to answer it.

Mandy swayed out of the hall and crossed the back of the couch that was near the entryway to get to the door. When she pulled the door open, Cherie couldn't believe who was standing there, flailing her arms open to embrace her cousin. This bitch had a lot of nerve.

"You smell good," Jessica excitedly said as she pulled away from Mandy. "Let me guess… Juicy Couure?"

"Close. Viva La Juicy," she giggled. "Let me grab my purse and we can get out of here. I had to make sure that my makeup was right before we left."

"And where the fuck are *y'all* going?" Cherie asked with attitude. Her eyes sliced through Mandy's while she waited for an answer.

"Just… out with the guys."

"And you think that's completely appropriate?"

"Rie—"

"Look at my fuckin' leg, Amanda! You couldn't stay behind just to make sure that I was going to be okay, at least?"

"You're grown—"

Cherie whipped her head around to Jessica and eyed her. Yes, Jessica was well-put together in her cowl neck sweater, leggings and black over the knee suede boots, but she was still no match for Mon Cherie. She couldn't help but to notice, up close, how much she reminded Cherie a lot of herself. They both had cherubic faces that could easily have make-up brushed onto them that would classify them as baddies, their bodies were both hourglass figures with cinched waists, and their natural hair was long and had good texture. Shane must've had good taste in women, especially to have two of them that were almost mirrored images of one another.

"Nice to meet you, Cherie," Jessica said, breaking the silence. "Shane has good taste, doesn't he?"

"And what does that mean?" Cherie worked her neck as she folded her arms to eye the young woman some more.

"I'm saying that you're beautiful without a speck of makeup on, or an extension in her head. Girl, you're dressed in sweats and a t-shirt and you're killing the game right now."

"I don't speak Ratchet-nese."

"Is she for real?" Jessica asked Mandy.

"Don't worry about her," Mandy replied. "Let it be water off a duck's back."

"Was it water off a duck's back when you called my house after-hours and I got my ass beat to be there for my family?" Cherie suddenly asked. "And was it water off a duck's back when you neglected to let me know that you were going to this bitch's baby shower?"

"I think you need to calm down," Jessica intervened.

"I'm talkin' to my cousin, bitch, this has nothing to do with you!"

"But you need to slow down on all of those bitches, alright? I gave you a compliment."

"I don't give a fuck about your compliment!"

"And now I see why it was that Shane came crawling back to me." Jessica, seemingly stealing Cherie's infamous hair-flip, flipped her hair over her shoulder and opened the front door. Before stepped over the threshold, she looked back at Mandy and said, "I'll be waiting inside the i8 in front of the house, Mandy. You know... the car that Shane *didn't* buy."

Cherie, for the moment, seemed as if she only sat in shock. Patiently, she waited for Mandy to leave the house before she booked a room, called her cellphone provider to change her number, and found an Uber so that she could leave. She didn't want to stick around for the bullshit.

With all of her things packed in luggage, boxes, and trash bags, she couldn't wait to take her pain medication because her leg felt like it was on fire. Everyone would soon regret overlooking her. She wouldn't regret leaving.

By the time that dessert was almost finished, Shane couldn't stop looking at Jessica as if she was the most gorgeous woman that he had ever seen. Over the past week, he had done one hell of a job to erase Cherie. He had pulled his goons off of Terry and paid them off. He put the house that he built for Cherie up for sale in hopes that he would come across another that he could purchase and raise his family in. Also, he blocked Cherie's number and erased it and all of their messages and call logs. To him, if it was out of sight then it would've been out of mind. For seven days, he practiced learning Jessica, and saw a lot about her that he liked and could get used to.

For instance, just before she would hit him, or restrain herself from doing so, she would crinkle her nose and stifle a smile. She was actually a pretty cool chick to be around, and he couldn't get enough of her. He also noticed that she would tap her fork or spoon on the edge of her plate before she would shove it into her mouth. She was very particular, just like him.

After dinner was over, it was almost as if Mandy and Jessica had forgotten about Cherie being rude and having an attitude, with how everybody's spirits had been lifted. Shane had escorted Jessica out to the curb and dapped Rich up before he and Mandy went their own way. While waiting for her car, Shane wrapped his arms around Jessica from behind and lightly swayed with her.

"What are you up to?" Jessica lightly giggled. Her hands coursed his over her abdomen.

"Nothing," he grumbled in her ear.

"De'Shane, I know you. What you got goin' on in that head of yours?"

"*Nothing*," he chuckled. "I'm just having a good time with you, Jessie. You let your walls down, and I'm glad that you did. You're not snotty to me anymore, and all I can do is show you how much I'm sorry for things that's happened in the past."

"Yea, well… speaking of the past. I met Cherie today."

Even hearing her name, it didn't make Shane let her go or become angry.

"At first, I thought she was beautiful, but homegirl is workin' with some demons over there."

"Don't worry about her. This is about us, and getting back into that place where we were before I started to act like a damn child. All you wanted me to do was grow up. So, here I am. I'm not finished with rebuilding myself yet, but you get to watch me, at least."

"I can give you that much." She kissed the underpart of his chin.

His phone vibrated in his pocket, and he rolled his eyes at it. He only hoped that Erykah wasn't the subject of the phone call. Reaching into his pocket, he tightened his grip around Jessica with his free hand before answering. "Yea?"

"Daddy needs to see us," Alyssa told him. "He has the DNA results back. Don't ask why it was mailed in a box and sent by UPS, but he just got them. We're meeting up at the big house."

"I gotchu. I'm about to be out in a minute."

"You with Jessie Pooh?"

"You know it," he chuckled.

"Rub her belly for me, and tell my niece or nephew that they're going to get the best aunt out of me. I swear."

"Layin' it on kind of thick, don't you think?"

"Shut up. Mama J said for you to hurry up."

"Consider me on my way." He hung up and looked down at Jessica's cocked brow. "Relax, babe," he told her with a smile. "It's family matters."

"Family, huh?" she questioned.

"It's cool. I gotta grow up a little more to slide a rock on your finger to make you family."

"I'll take that, but you need to remember to get some sleep, De'Shane."

Her car finally arrived at the curb, and Shane gave her a kiss on the cheek, then one on her lips that almost made her knees weak.

"You know I'm gonna get some sleep. Anything to keep you happy, baby."

"Mhhmm." She rolled her eyes and accepted her keys from the valet. "Let me know what happens with the fam."

"I will, baby. And Jess?"

She stopped before she could get into the i8 and looked over the roof of her car at him.

"I love you."

"I love you too, Shane," she blushed.

He tapped the roof of the car with his bottom lip tucked between his teeth before he jogged around the corner to his Jaguar.

After Jessica was seated and was about to pull off, she couldn't shake the look that Cherie had. She was resting on the fact that they looked so much alike, that Shane only chose her to remind him of the woman he lost so long ago. She had to shake it off to try and enjoy the Shane of hers that wasn't a beast or a screaming maniac who didn't mind reminding you what he was capable of.

CHAPTER SIX

The Legacies

Shane got out of the Jaguar and took off his leather bomber, and threw it in the backseat. When he shut the door, he checked his prized Conway Kosso watch. The only reason that it was prized was because Shane was a collector of unique things that others didn't have, and Jessica had gotten it for him during their shopping trip a week ago. This specific time piece had modern detailing with custom knurling on both the bezel and wrist line. It was woodgrain with stainless steel links and clasp. The midnight blue face of it complimented his cotton dress shirt and the polka dots in his white bowtie. Seeing that it was a little after eight and that his sisters' cars were out front, he put his midnight blue, suede Gucci loafers that were designed with an elongated toe, to work and went inside to see what the hell was going on now. Hopefully, he wouldn't have to hold anybody back, and luckily for him, Quita had already braided his dreads into two fishbone braids, and connected them at the nape of his neck into one long braid down his back. He wiped his face with his hand before going into the Big House, and was instantly greeted by Erykah when he pushed the door open.

She eyed him and stood back for a second. "Who you lookin' all good for?" she asked.

"I should be asking you the same thing," he joked. Secretly, he complimented her navy-blue cocktail dress and matching heels with golden scorpions over the toes of them.

"Had a date and it didn't go too well," she explained. "It's cool though. The dude didn't even open the door for me, pull out my chair, or take my order for me. Damn, I let him take charge and he didn't. And this, my brother, is why I can't keep a man. Some of 'em don't know how to be one."

"Okay, y'all!" they heard Mama J call. "Come gather 'round! We need to read over these before Darius leaves!"

"Who?" Erykah asked her brother.

"The lawyer," Shane chuckled. He then hooked his arm within hers and promised, "When this is over, we can go for a drink to make up for your date. Just you and me. I mean, we're already damn near dressed alike, and something tells me that we're going to need a drink after this."

When they left the foyer and arrived in the sitting room, Apollo was sitting in his wheelchair with his head slumped back while Mama J adjusted his neck pillow. It was clear that he was on some type of sedative with the way his eyes were drooping and it barely looked as if he had made eye contact with even her.

Ashington wiped away a falling tear as Darius stood in his skinny pantsuit with a set of papers in his hands, and Quita gripped Alyssa's hand tight. They were sitting on the couch while Ash took her seat on the arm of it. Shane seated Erykah in the tall-back chair near the fireplace and hitched up the legs of his pants to sit on the faint couch beside it.

"All of my babies," Apollo lowly said with a weak smile, though his voice was choppy.

Mama J rolled her eyes up to the ceiling to keep her tears at bay, but it wasn't working. The day after tomorrow would be Jazz's funeral, and she didn't know how much more she could pretend to be so strong for the sake of the family.

"Now, we're going to get to it, you guys," Darius said, adjusting his circular-framed glasses on his face. He readied the pages in his hands as everyone braced themselves. "In the case of Ashington Taylor-Cruz…"

She gulped and held her breath altogether. It would've killed her to know that Apollo cherished his baby girl more than anything on the planet, but she wasn't his blood or the fruit from his loins.

"According to the blood test and mouth swab that you had taken in Augusta, Georgia… Apollo Cruz *is* your father, by ninety-nine-point-nine percent."

She let go of all of the wind in her body and dropped her head. Quita wrapped her arms around her baby sister and squeezed her a little for comfort.

"In the case of Alyssa London…"

Alyssa held her head high and stood up in case she had to give her a dad a hug. In the event that she wasn't his child, she didn't want him to fly off into a raving fit, and have her mother murdered.

"According to the blood test and mouth swab that you had taken in Augusta, Georgia… Apollo Cruz *is* your father, by ninety-nine-point-nine percent."

A lone tear streamed down her cheek as she slowly took her seat. She then looked to Apollo and gave him a weak smile. "See, daddy," she mustered. "I'm a better daughter. Much better."

He lightly nodded at her. He couldn't get his words together.

Shane's phone vibrated in his pocket. He quickly snagged it so that he could see what the problem could've been. Only… there was none. It was just Jessica, letting him know that she made it home and that she was wanting to know if everything was okay.

"In the case of Jazmine Cruz; may she rest in peace…" Darius continued, while Shane sent his text.

Shane had to stop and look up at him over his long and dramatic pause. Everyone in the room had held their breaths. She was the main the reason that they had taken the tests in the first place, so finding out that she wasn't Apollo's kid could be damaging.

"According to the blood test and mouth swab that she had taken in Augusta, Georgia… Apollo Cruz *is* her father, by ninety-nine-point-nine percent."

Silently, they all cheered and thanked God. They only wished that she could've been there to see and hear the results herself.

"In the case of Marquita White-Cruz…"

Quita crossed her legs as she waited for an answer. She was all too confident that her daddy was hers.

"According to the blood test and mouth swab that you had taken in Augusta, Georgia… Apollo Cruz is *not* your father, by ninety-nine-point-nine percent."

The gasps erupted and Quita's face hardened. It took her some time to look over at her father. When their eyes connected, tears started to stream down her cheeks. There was nothing that she could say.

"It's not your fault," Mama J assured her, with her cheeks glistening as well. "Your mama lied to you, Quita, but it don't mean that Apollo ain't your daddy, ya' hear?"

"Yea, Quita," Ashington agreed. "You're still *my* sister." She then laid her head on Quita's shoulder and hugged her.

Shane texted Jessica to let her know what had happened, and only prayed that Erykah's results wouldn't come back the same.

"In the case of Erykah Cruz…" Darius went on.

Apollo tried to squeeze Joyce's hand as much as he could, because Erykah was considered his first born. To find that she wasn't his, it would break his heart in more ways than one. He always wanted Joyce, but he could never get the wife he chased after. His line of work prevented that, even though it was his own daughter who came looking for him and placed he and who he considered his woman back into each other's lives.

Shane stopped texting and reached over to grab Erykah's hand. She wasn't at all afraid until she felt her brother's digits slip through her own. She locked eyes with him, and it reminded her of older times when she was about to do something dangerous, or wanted to stick her chest out and couldn't. Shane would always look her deep in the eyes and say, "Keep your eyes on me, Rick. Watch me, and do the damn thing. I'm giving you strength, girl." Thinking of it made the big bad diva tilt her head and release a tear to dance down the side of her beat face.

"Eye's on me," Shane lowly demanded. "I'm still your big brother, Rick. Look at me."

She complied with her heart pounding faster and faster because of Darius' pause.

He finally shifted the pages and pushed his glasses up on the bridge of his nose. "According to the blood test and mouth swab that you had taken in Augusta, Georgia… Apollo Cruz *is* your father, by ninety-nine-point-nine percent."

She could've fallen out of her seat when Shane let her hand go.

Apollo, on the other hand, squeezed Joyce's hand a little tighter. "I knew you were always a good woman, Joyce," he said with a raspy voice.

"Still am," she laughed through her tears.

Shane picked his phone up off his knee to check his messages, and to reply to them. Because of it, and thinking that it was over— not at all remembering that he had taken a DNA test as well— he had gone deaf to whatever else Darius had to say.

"In the case of De'Shane Heartford…" Darius spewed. "According to the blood test and mouth swab that you had taken in Augusta, Georgia… Apollo Cruz *is* your father, by ninety-nine-point-nine percent."

Erykah's breathing stopped again. All heads swiveled between Shane and Apollo, trying to figure out how it was even possible that Shane could've been his son.

"Shane," Erykah called her brother.

He hadn't answered. He was so deep into his response to his emotional, pregnant woman that he hadn't even heard her.

"De'Shane!" Mama J bellowed from across the room.

Finally, he looked up with his mouth wide open. "I'm sorry, mama, what?"

"You didn't hear what was just said?"

"Yea," he shrugged. "My daddy ain't my daddy."

"Brother, that's not what was said," Ash told him.

"What?" he chuckled. "Why wouldn't it be?"

Every eye in the sitting room went to Apollo then, including Shane's. They needed to know how he adopted someone who was in his bloodline.

He tapped the tip of his pointer-finger on the arm of his wheelchair while he sorted through his thoughts. "I remember her. Michelle, I mean," he explained. "It was a block party when I had her. She looked much different though, and it was before she was paralyzed. She was a... a hoodrat. I thought she was easy, she wanted it, and I gave it to her in the back of my limo. Never did I think of it. She never told me she was pregnant. Ever. I mean, some of y'all mamas threatened to keep you away from me because I didn't want to be with them, but Michelle... she never came to me. Had I known, I would've tried to co-parent, just like I tried with the others. I guess it was just fate that she came to me, wanting me to adopt you, Shane."

"You're not mad, are you, brother?" Quita asked.

"No," he said breathlessly and surprisingly. "How can I be?"

"Shane, are you sure?" Erykah asked at his side.

"Very. I mean, you weren't there for the first twelve years of my life, but I got you eventually. Now ain't the time to point fingers or try to figure out why my mama didn't open her mouth, or why y'all didn't take precaution. I have my family, that's all I need."

"Who the fuck are you and what have you done with my brother?"

He looked at her and smiled. "I'm growing up."

"Growing up, my ass! Mama, can we eat?"

"Wait a second," Apollo said. He pulled Joyce by her hand to make her stand in front of him. He looked up into her eyes, and with his words slurring and all, he proclaimed, "Look at all these kids, Joyce."

She burst into laughter through her tears.

"You didn't have to help me keep them together, or help to keep their mamas in line, but you did. You never had to do anything that you've done for me, and I'm sorry that I could never be the man you wanted me to be. But Joyce, I ain't got much time left. You think you can find it in your heart to take the hand of a hood legend, with all these kids that he got?" From underneath the black velvet blanket over his legs, he retrieved a golden box and handed it to her.

She accepted it and opened it, knowing that he couldn't do it himself. The ring inside took her breath away. She clasped her hand over her mouth and took a sloppy step back.

"So, what do you say? We can do this thing in a couple of days and kick off whatever else is about to happen. Joyce, if I'm gonna go, I want to go a happy man. I got all my kids, and I don't give a fuck what DNA says. Even though I've lost one, I understand why she took herself away. But I don't think I'm gonna be able to handle you being away from me anymore than what you have been."

"Mama!" Erykah called. "You better stop playin' and give my daddy a chance! I've dreamed of this moment since I reconnected y'all!"

"Yes," Joyce finally squealed. "I will, Apollo. Yes, I will marry you!"

Her answer brought about smiles and applause, and nothing else mattered in the moment.

To Shane, it proved that life was too short and that redemption was possible.

The Cruz siblings wandered through the house after celebrating the engagement of the only real mother that they've known and their father. It was safe to say that every heart in the home was light, and they were all taking trips down Memory Lane. Shane jogged up the stairs to his old room, and pet the family dog's bronze statue when he turned the corner. Then, he located his room at the end of the hall, and opened the pair of Victorian styled doors that had his name embedded in the wood. When they were younger, he and Erykah thought that it would've been cool to have all of their names on the outside of their doors to let any visitor know whose room belonged to who, and to somehow show that they had class enough to mark their territory.

Inside of his old room, Shane took a deep breath and inhaled the cinnamon scent of the Glade plug-in somewhere within his domain. Since he was a boy, he was used to the cleaning service coming into the home every Wednesday and Sunday to tidy up the place. Yet, it was still Shane's responsibility to keep his room and laundry in tip-top shape.

He sat on the couch at the foot of his bed and looked at his closet, just next to his fireplace, and smirked. He remembered the first time that he jogged down the steps from his room to go to an event with his father. Apollo saw a wrinkle in his black dress shirt and backhanded Shane so hard that he hit the wall closest to him, bounced off it, and landed on his side.

"No child of mine is sloppy," Apollo seemingly growled.

Erykah, standing in the distance, slapped her hand over her mouth and trembled at what had happened. She had just met her father a few months prior and begged and pleaded to stay for a weekend.

Apollo didn't take it easy on his baby girl either. He strong-eyed her to make sure that she was pristine. Her dress with a tutu skirt was well-put together, and her flesh colored stocking didn't have a run in them. But the man who paid attention to detail as his son had, found something wrong. "Go change your shoes, girl, and with haste," he demanded. "No reason you should have a fuckin' scuff on 'em. I just bought 'em!"

Erykah flinched, just before helping Shane up off the marble floor to take flight with him up the stairs. He helped her go through her massive closet and collection of new shoes to find something suitable to wear to the dinner party that was oh so important to their father.

Then, with her flats in hand, she ran to Shane's room to locate his iron while he struggled to hurriedly get out of his dress shirt, so that she could quickly run an iron over it. Their bond, on that day, was sealed. No one could ever tell the two that they weren't each other's ride-or-dies.

Over time, they learned their father because of that one incident. They learned that he was dirt poor in Augusta and that what he did gain, he cherished. He had long come from wearing or obtaining hand-me-downs from his siblings. He was far from living in a two-bedroom shack. He taught his children the same: preserve what you have and take pride in it. Even though he swung an iron fist to prove his point, his kids understood.

Whereas he wasn't abusive toward the girls, if Shane stepped out of line, he could expect a backhand to the face or fist in the chest. He had to rebuild the boy to make him a man. He had to reach in and pull out all of Shane's bad habits and throw them away. Because of Apollo, Shane was no longer a slouch, or lanky. He was no longer a procrastinator and cared more about his studies. In fact, the majority of the time that Shane appeared to only text on his phone, he was actually on his Microsoft Word app, preparing or closing a paper. He learned long ago to balance work, family and his schooling. Apollo wouldn't have it any other way. Shane wasn't allowed to have a bachelor's degree. Apollo made him strive for higher. He made Shane promise to achieve his master's, and Shane obliged. He had two more years left in college, and he didn't plan on stopping. Especially now that his father's time was dwindling, he couldn't wait to dedicate his masters' in business, political science, and mathematics in his father's honor.

Having enough of skipping down the path to what was, he rose from the couch at the foot of his king size bed and went into Erykah's room, only four doors down and toward the stairs from his own. She hated for her siblings just to barge in, but Shane, as he said, was a god. He didn't have to listen to her or take her feelings into consideration. He ignored her on the phone with her colleague and slid across her made canopy bed to try and disturb the starched sheets on purpose.

She sneered at him and turned her back to him to finish her phone call. "Well, this was not my idea to open up a new damn shop, Quinndalin," she complained. "It was a premature move, and I said that after I had gone over the books. Yea, we could afford the building and renovation, but we weren't going to be able to afford all the material we needed for more stock, and you put your hand into this. So, you know what? It's going to be your money that goes into it… You're what?… Well, that's not my problem. I'll just get the documents together to cease and desist, because I don't tolerate misrepresenting funds, or whatever the fuck you just called it." She hung up and plopped down on the edge of her bed with her arms folded. "I can use that drink now, brother," she said to him.

"What was that about, Rick?" He rolled over onto his back and grabbed a pillow from the head of the bed to toy with it.

"My so-called partner," she grumbled. "She went against what I said to open up another boutique. She didn't think about stock or nothing else, and the bitch was spending my money, swearing that it was ours."

"So, what? You need dough?"

"You know damn well that I'm not gonna ask anybody for anything."

Since she was seventeen, Erykah made jewelry for her friends. By her senior year of high school, she didn't need Apollo to pay for anything, with her income being a profit of almost $800 in a month. She was making twice as much as some of her friends who were pushing minimum-waged jobs, and she didn't have to punch a clock. Many wondered where her money came from and many still hadn't known. She wasn't the face of her company. She had two models for that. Her passion, as she called it, was "putting together shiny and brand new trinkets to slay the game." That's all she wanted to do. Her custom pieces were worn even by her own brother. With his allowance, Shane would fork over almost $400 for Erykah to put him together a ring, a watch, a bracelet, a necklace, or all of the above. When she moved on from cubic zirconia and bumped up to diamonds, Shane must've pushed all of his sister's clientele out of the way to receive her very first custom piece and he didn't care about it. In fact, he reached out to Erykah to create Cherie's angel wing pendent and the bracelet that he had given back to her. Erykah put her foot in the designs, and even though he hated to give the beautiful piece to Cherie, he had meaning behind why he did it.

None of Apollo's children were lazy or had to call their daddy for money. Quita had a beauty and barber shop in downtown Richmond, and she didn't need him to fork over the money to open or renovate. Jazmine, before her death, had her own art gallery where she would display her hand-painted works or enlarged portraits of different areas of the city that she photographed. Her work sold for thousands. Alyssa, even on hard times and battling a bad habit, might've been a corner girl, but she didn't have a pimp and she didn't call her father for what she needed. Ashington's hustle has been and still is selling her notes, footnotes, or answers to exams and tests. Apollo being a distant co-parent still instilled the power of the hustle in his children, and it was one thing that he could say that he was truly proud of.

Erykah huffed and laid back on the bed next to her brother, crossing her legs so that no one could come in and see her bloomers underneath her dress. "This bitch done gone and opened up a whole other boutique, brother," she said lowly. "I'm the sole proprietor. How could she even do that without my consent? And now I'm missing a hunnit and twenty-five stacks over this shit. She took money out of my fund to do this shit. All I have left seventy-five grand. What the fuck am I going to do? I can't afford the shipment that's coming in, in two months. Those diamonds, silver and gold, is going to cost me damn near three-hundred grand. After profit over the next two months, I was going to be able to afford it. Now I'm takin' a hit. What do I do, Baby Apollo?"

It hadn't taken Shane long to calculate and to figure out a solution. That's exactly why he was chose to be adopted by his own father in the first place. "Well, make it a sub company," he offered. "Make her ass pay for half the jewels and metal. Draw up a contract that discloses so. Make her pay you sixty percent of profit until she's given you your money back. Your spot can still be exclusive, the way you've been wanting it to be. With a sub company, you can promote that as well, and push that bitch to get more money. Can't be mad at two sources of income, Rick."

She playfully punched him the arm with a smile on her face, and stared up at the ceiling of her bed. "I knew you were around for a reason."

"I told you from the day that I met you that I got you. You're my sister, Rick. Why wouldn't I make sure that you're okay?"

"I don't like this sentimental ass version of you," she complained as she rose from the bed. "Can we go and get that drink? And call your baby mama. Lord knows that she's ready to pop."

"Whatever," he chuckled. "You'll love me, dammit!"

CHAPTER SEVEN

All Of The Light

After Jazz's somber and small funeral, the siblings only recalled the good times that they had with her. Especially the first time that Apollo had all six of his kids in the same home for a weekend. No matter what so-called work he had to do with being the plug for Virginia and surrounding states, he never left his kids hanging when it came time to be together. Father and family time was that important to him.

The first-time Jazz was at the Big House with them, she spoke so softly and so quietly that they all kept having to yell, "What?" to her, to get her to speak up. Still, Erykah reigned supreme as the most vociferous of the bunch. As the middle child, Jazz was so gentle and fragile. Luckily, she had siblings to protect her and to keep harm and offense as far away from her as possible, but they didn't know that her own mother was the culprit of Jazz's mental abuse. Had they known, their sister would still be alive and well.

Then, it was time to celebrate the union between Joyce and

91

Apollo. They chose to have their wedding very small and intimate. A few of Apollo's colleagues were in attendance, as was Joyce's immediate family. All of the girls cried in the audience with everyone else because it was a fairytale come true. The beast of Richmond was wedding his beauty, and it took death to finally make Joyce tear down her walls and submit. What she hadn't known was that even though he was sick, nothing at all had changed about the man that she once was willing to go to war for. That night, she had to refrain from calling someone and tell them how well he still performed over their honeymoon, even though all he did was lay on his back.

However, life still moved on within the following three weeks. Especially for Terry. He decided to snitch against the mafia to salvage his own freedom. Yet and still, he wanted his Cherie. He used what money he could access within protective custody to send someone to Richmond with multiple photos of her, from different angles. When he received word that she was pregnant, it made Terry *furious*. He knew there was a reason that she was wanting to go back to Virginia. He just wanted to know how long she had been fucking De'Shane behind his back. What he didn't know is that his spy caught the wrong girl, and only thought that it was Cherie. From the distance, in the photo on funeral grounds, Jessica looked a little too much like Cherie, only with black hair, and you could tell that she was around four months pregnant. Only, everyone around had already known that Jessica was not as early as she appeared to be. Terry, on the other hand, was completely fooled when staring at the photo of the young woman with oversized black shades on her face, pulling Shane along by the hand. The bangs she wore didn't help any either when it came to verifying if she was Cherie or not. Terry had all the proof he needed that there wasn't a mix-up. She was the same height, same build, she was with Shane and she looked to be trying to conceal her pregnancy. He should've thought of seeing her in her bathing suit before she left five weeks prior. There was no way she could've grown a belly in that amount of time.

Still, with tears cascading down his cheeks, he picked up his cellphone and ordered, "When you get a clear shot... kill her ass. That Shane nigga, too. Make them *bleed*."

If only Cherie had heard the threat. She walked, without a limp, into Royal Six boutique, after responding to an email for a managerial and sales position on Craig's List. She politely waited at the front counter, constantly checking her reflection to make sure that she didn't have a hair out of place in her tight bun. Her leg was screaming for her to get off it and to go back to the condo she newly rented so that she could take her pain pills, yet she was persistent to make something of her new lonely life.

Erykah saw her on the security camera and raised from the seat behind her desk to see what the hell Cherie was doing in her shop. She approached the counter with her brows pressed tightly together. "Hey, Cherie," she spoke. "What brings you by?"

"Hey," she nervously sang. "I'm here for an interview. I corresponded with someone by the name of Quinndalin?"

"You have got to be shitting me." Erykah dropped her head to get her words in order before she spoke again. Then, she swiped her full locks behind her head and looked up at the beauty in front of her. "She was supposed to send you to her shop, but I guess God works in mysterious ways. Do you have a resume?"

"I don't actually…"

"Okay, any sales experience?"

"No, but I have the gift of gab."

"Cherie, I didn't want to stereotype you, but I don't think I have a choice right now. You haven't had a job before, have you?"

Shyly, she shook her head.

"Alright," Erykah huffed. "Look, I can't be here all the time, and I was going to put out an ad for a new employee anyway. I guess Quinndalin just wanted me to interview you and check you out first. *But…* I ain't sending you to her. I want the best. What I need for you to do is sell as much as you can in a day, alright? Other than that, just smile and look good. Custom pieces need to be ran by the designer. He's only here on Wednesdays, so book them an appointment for the coming Wednesday after they come in. Can you do that?"

"I can."

"And you can count, right?"

"Right."

"Good. Can you come back tomorrow so I can go over everything else in greater detail?"

"I sure can."

"Okay. Well, congratulations, you have a job. Just don't fuck this up because of whatever beef you got goin' with my brother."

Cherie started to say something back, but she needed this job more than she needed to argue or to so-called clear her name. Besides, for every piece she sold, she read in the email that she would receive a ten percent commission.

On her way back to the hotel in a Prius that she snagged from a car lot a week prior, she decided to stop at a lounge to get a drink. She took a seat on the stool at the bar and waited for the bartender to make his way down to her. To consume her time, she fished through her purse for her phone and checked her Facebook account. She made sure to delete and block people who wouldn't contribute to her movement.

"What can I get for you, Miss?" the bartender asked.

The tone he used caused Cherie to looked up at him with raised brows. That voice of his gave her a shiver, and the soothing baritone in it made her tighten her thighs. She just had to see who he was with a voice like his.

The bartender had a nice Caesar fade and his teeth were strong and pearly white. She could tell with the way he flashed his clean set at her. The chocolate brother must've been an athlete of some sort, because his chest was pushing at the fabric of his dark purple dress shirt. With the top two buttons undone, she could see a tattoo along his collarbone, peek-a-booing from underneath the white muscle shirt that was exposed there. To her, he didn't look like a regular old bartender.

"Umm… can I get a mango margarita?" she shyly asked.

"Coming right up, beautiful." He had given her a wink to retrieve her drink.

While waiting, she browsed her newsfeed and gathered that she needed more friends. Everyone on Facebook seemed to be a little bummy. Either they were depressed or searching for religious answers.

A call had come through on her phone, and it was a number that she didn't recognize. Knowing that no one had the new number, she answered in case it was a job posting that she answered to. "Yes?"

"Cherie?" Erykah called her.

"Yea, it's me."

"Hey. Can you wear black and silver tomorrow? You're already a bad bitch, so I don't really need to instruct you much."

"Sure."

"Be here at eight. You'll have lunch from eleven to one, and then open back up at one-fifteen. You're off at five. Your salary will be a grand and a half a month, plus commission. Is that okay?"

It wasn't like she had a choice. Out of her personal stash, she only had close to $20,000 left after the down payment on the Prius, new clothes, and six months' rent on the condo. "Of course, that's fine," she said eagerly.

"That means that you're going to have to work your ass off for that commission."

"Believe me when I say that I'm ready."

"I hope so. See you at eight, chick."

Cherie hung up the phone and went to her Instagram account. She created a whole new one and added different people in what was her inner-circle back in California, simply because she knew that they had money. She made her profile picture a diamond and made the handle out to be "Love_JewelsXOXO".

"Here you are, gorgeous," the bartender said, sliding her margarita closer to her. "I forgot to ask you if you wanted salt or sugar, so I took it upon myself to add sugar. You look like you would've preferred something as sweet as you."

"I did, actually," she giggled.

He showcased his impressive grill again before he vanished, but that wouldn't be the last time she saw him.

By her third drink, they were laughing and talking up a storm. He hated to be rude to tend to his other customers, so he gave Cherie his cellphone number and made her promise to call him when she made it to her new condo. She had, and even then, she couldn't stop smiling from his one-liners and the way he made fun of some of her troubles. She had learned that he was twenty-five, single with no kids, and the bartending gig he held down was only during the day. By night, he was an exotic dancer. She started to ask him if that's the only thing he wanted to do until he disclosed that he made an average of three grand in tips and wages bi-weekly. Sometimes he would leave one party, gathering or club just to head to another, but he would never stay out past two in the morning. The lounge he worked in was family-owned, so he could quit if he wanted, but he didn't want to leave his uncle and cousins hanging with the labor. It took Cherie all of three hours talking to him during his shift over the phone to find out that his name was Damon. He even invited her out to the club that he would be working in the following Friday night, and she agreed.

To celebrate getting a new job, she sent Erykah a text that said that she was taking her out, and that it was Cherie's treat. She told

Erykah to even invite Quita. Lowkey, Cherie was being petty. Even if they liked little Miss Jessica, she was determined to show the both of them her good attributes like her loving to have fun and let loose. Using his sisters, it would cause some friction and make Shane remember who she was, since he wanted to hand her back pieces of jewelry that was supposed to mean something to the both of them. She knew how to hurt him, and it wasn't with weapons or words. He was once emotionally dependent on her, and she was going to use it in her favor.

The next morning, Cherie was in front of Royal Six's bright and early. Erykah arrived with some gossip that Cherie enjoyed, even though she didn't know who the people were that were in the situation. Erykah taught her how to work the register, how to keep the stock, and how to open and close the vault where she held pieces for clients who needed their jewelry cleaned or reshaped. By noon, she found herself inside the lounge's restroom with Damon, loving the feel of his abs against her own. Hell, she had a two-hour lunch so you could say that she used it very wisely. She just couldn't stand the sweet, sexy and goofy texts that he was sending her throughout the day and the night prior, so she swore that he would have to put his lips and dick to use since he made her want him.

He pleased her in a way that no one else had. In the private restroom, inside his uncle's office, he had Cherie sitting on the edge of the sink, after he made sure that her insides were explored. With his lips cupped around her clit, and the soft suckles that he was using, it caused an overflow of juices. Damon didn't hesitate to drink from her fountain. After making sure that she was properly drained of energy and cleansed with his tongue, he helped her to her Prius and kissed her full on the lips. He told her not to forget about the event on that Friday, and reminded her to bring her friends. She assured him that she would, and bid him a good afternoon.

When she strutted into Royal Six's, Erykah stood off the stool behind the counter when getting a look at how different Cherie's hair was. When she left, it was in a long and sleek ponytail, and now it was over both her shoulders.

"Homegirl, you ain't slick," Erykah said, wiggling her finger. "Who you got some noon dick from?"

"What?" Cherie giggled. "I don't know what you're talking about."

"You know damn well what I'm talking about. You're tripping over your six inches, your hips are swaying a little more wildly, and your hair was in a damn ponytail when you left for lunch. Like I said... who did you get some high noon dick from?"

"Oh my God, Erykah. I can't talk to you about things like this."

"Spill all the juice. Fuck tea. Hell, it ain't like Shane is worried about you, and you damn sure ain't worried about him."

The remark stung a little, but she weaved it and kept it pushing. Cherie waddled into the back to pull off her heels and exchange them for flats. When she had come back, the bitch that made her snarl was standing there, speaking to Erykah with a silver watch in her hand.

"You have to fix it before he loses his damn mind," Jessica stressed. "The last thing I want him to do is be mad over a gift that I fucking broke."

Cherie smirked when thinking that Jessica would get into trouble over something that Shane had given her.

An older gentleman stepped into the shop, and Cherie took that as her chance to do her job for the first time that day.

"Welcome to Royal Six's, sir," she said soothingly with a smile. "How can I help you today? Anything in particular that you're looking for?"

When the gentleman looked up, he couldn't help but to stare at Cherie and squint. He had to adjust the thin rectangular frames on his face to get a better look at her. He had the most striking brown eyes that she had ever seen. They looked so familiar to her.

"Are you okay, sir?" Cherie politely asked him, swallowing her own question of if they knew each other.

Cautiously, he looked over his shoulder at Jessica, then back at her. "What's your name?" he asked lowly.

"Mon Cherie," she giggled.

"Hhmm… interesting."

"Is everything okay, daddy?" Jessica asked the gentleman.

Cherie cocked her brow at Jessica and was ready to cuss her out, but she knew that she needed her job.

"Uh… yea," the man said. "I, uh… need a gift for my lovely daughter," he then told Cherie. "She's about to be a mom, and I want something that explains how much I love her."

Even though Cherie's stomach churned and her insides cringed, she showed the man to a gorgeous diamond tennis bracelet that had butterflies and bows dangling from it. She had even convinced him to grab the matching necklace since he loved his daughter as he claimed.

"Daddy, this is beautiful," Jessica gasped. "I love them both."

"Good," he chimed. "Young lady, please box them both and ring me up. My baby girl approves."

His smile most definitely was familiar to Cherie somehow. She tried her best to remember where she had seen him before. When he slid his credit card to her, she made a mental note of the name on it, and swiped it.

After bagging the expensive trinkets and sending the pair on their way, Erykah whispered, "Is it just me, or do y'all look alike?"

"Seriously?" Cherie grumbled.

"I appreciate the way you handled that, because if I was you, I would've drug her ass. I don't like her. Still don't like her. I beat that ass before, and if she ain't careful… I might drag her again after she has this baby."

"Why don't you like her?" Cherie asked curiously as she slid up on her stool.

"Her attitude. She gets in her ways where she thinks she's better than everybody else. Look, I worked as hard as she did if not harder to get to where I am. She likes to rub it in your face that her daddy has money and that she doesn't need it."

"So y'all are basically the same person?" Cherie's nose crinkled.

"Shut up," Erykah giggled. "But you see my point though? We're on the same fuckin' level, but she likes to be better. Let me tell you some real shit though, Rie," Erykah adjusted herself on the stool to fully face her, and crossed her legs. "There was an incident when she was a lawyer. I pushed her to her limits because I heard what she said about you, and I was tired of her competing. Now, at the time, I didn't know that you were real, so I was fed up with her thinking that she was competing with even a ghost. I had to put her in her damn place. She was just too much. Maybe she has something for Shane, but I still doubt that."

"Thanks… I think."

"Now… Where'd you get some dick from."

Cherie only gave Erykah a school girl like giggle before she straightened her strands with her fingers and left it at that. "Oh, you'll meet him Friday."

Shane wouldn't be happy to know that his Cherie had his sisters at the strip club, watching a half-naked man.

CHAPTER EIGHT

Bring On The Thunder

*D*ressed in a short black romper short-set, Erykah straightened her locks and had them over one shoulder. When she and Quita stepped out of her Mercedes, most of the women that were lined outside of the building could've been ridden with jealousy. It was dripping from their faces, and neither of the women could give two fucks about their opinions. Anytime the sisters had the chance to step out together, they always made sure to complement each other. Quita decided to wear a long and skinny ponytail with her sweetheart neckline, corseted top of her leather jumpsuit, with six-inch leather pumps. She just knew that she was the shit, and every other woman could gag on the BBW's beauty.

It didn't take them long to find Cherie next to the bouncer who held a velvet rope in his hand. She was dressed in a pair of short black shorts but wore a loose sequin, spaghetti strapped top with heels that matched. Her hair was in curls all over her head, and anyone would've thought that she stepped out of the 1970's with her style of choice for the night.

The group entered the noisy club and located the VIP table that faced the woodened tiles on the club's floor, which was sectioned off for the performances. Shortly after they sat, a waitress brought the women a bottle of Ace of Spades with a sparkler in a skinny vase next to it.

"Enjoy," the woman told them over the music with a smile. "You have more of those coming! Is there something that I can get you in the meantime?"

"Let me get a classic margarita," Quita said.

"Yea, and I'll have the same," Erykah added.

"Can you get me a Sex on the Beach?" Cherie asked. "And please… make it nasty."

The waitress nodded and left the group so that she could retrieve their orders.

"Let me find out that you have some nasty in you," Quita laughed from the other side of Erykah. "Let me taste that when you get it. I ain't ever had one of those."

"Girl, you don't know what you're missing! It's Malibu Rum with mango, strawberry and blueberry! When I tell you that it's the *perfect* mixture… it's an understatement!"

"I may have underestimated you, Cherie!"

"A lot of people do!"

Erykah poured their drinks and raised her glass in the air. "To fun after the storm!" she cheered.

"Much, much fun!" Cherie agreed.

They clinked glasses and let the night begin. They didn't expect three other dancers to appear before Cherie's boo, just like they didn't predict that they would have the time of their lives with handsome, sculpted men picking them up and doing tricks with them, all the while turning them on. It was so much happening that Erykah lost one of her shoes, Quita lost an earring and Cherie was so tipsy that she didn't even realize that she broke a nail with trying to pry her clutch open for a hundred-dollar bill so that she could get more ones for the stallions.

Finally, "Freak'in Me" by Jamie Foxx and Marsha Ambrosius played, and the lights in the club dimmed. The single spotlight was purple and it cast upon a 6'3" man who prowled his way from the back in a pair of black cargo pants, combat boots and a black V-neck shirt that clung to his upper-half. The shades on his face hid his eyes, but Cherie knew who he was.

"That's him!" Erykah squealed. "Girl, that's your noon dick!"

"P-Slayer... give it to 'em!" the DJ screamed over the mic.

When Damon dropped to the floor and grind against it, the women in the audience couldn't wait for him to take his clothes off. They threw bills at him because of his stroke alone.

"Oooh, baby, just take somethin' off!" Quita begged.

Damon slithered his way over to the table on his knees and, slickly, lifted Cherie's left leg over his shoulder, kissed her inner thigh, then brought the right leg up. Without her being prepared, he stood with her, and kissed the seat of her shorts without anyone else being able to see. She was so hot and ready that she didn't hear the women screaming at Damon's strength.

He took her to the middle of the floor and eased her down on to her feet. On the outside, Cherie was cool. Inside, however, she was begging for his set to be over so that he could meet her back at her condo. Damon took off his shirt and all hell broke loose. The lights in the club came up just a tad and the spotlight turned white, to showcase the cuts, dents and curves of his abs, chest, arms and back. Quickly, he spun Cherie around and forced to spread her legs and bend over. Women in the crowd should've run out of money over that one incident with how they threw out more bills when Damon animatedly ground against Cherie's massive backside. The illusion of sex was worth it because Damon made sure to pay the rent to his condo on this night.

He spotted Erykah and beckoned her with his finger. Afterward, he laid a passionate kiss on Cherie's neck that told her to be ready after his job was done because she was going to get it.

Erykah was hesitant about getting up, but she did so, and Damon folded and flipped her into so many positions that it was pitiful. She was only grateful that she could just have Quita to re-do her hair if need be. Then, it was Quita's turn. By then, "Take You Down" by Chris Brown was playing, and he had to make an example out of the chunky miss. He snagged a chair from the crowd and sat her in it. He made sure to give Quita the best lap dance of her life, and even unbuttoned and unzipped his pants, pulled them off, tossed them, and let her see his package up close and personal. Quita could've passed out at it. At the climax of the song, he had taken her out of the chair, laid her down on the wooden floor, and dove to grind on her. Quita was blinded by the cash, but she reckoned that it was time to get some dick after their dance. She was going to have to pull out her little black book and make a phone call for someone discreet, and who wouldn't bother her when all was said and done.

After the performance, every girl had to waddle to their cars with smiles on their faces. Eryah had to take off her last shoe and keep it in her hand.

"Rie!" Quita sang her name as she walked. "Girl, I ain't had fun like that in a long ass time. I got to give it to you. It was worth it. And that P-Slayer is your new boo?"

"I wouldn't take it that far," she giggled. "I'll put it to you like this. He's knocking the kinks out that your brother left me with."

"That nigga. I got to get to the crib, have somebody knock out my kinks, and get some sleep. I got to get up early to re-dye his hair and twist it up in a different style. Y'all know that Shane tha God doesn't like tardiness."

"I'm glad you had fun, Quita. All bullshit aside, I had to make a truce with you since I'm going to be living in Richmond, and because I'm going to be working with Erykah. Besides, we started off on the wrong foot."

"We did! And congrats on the new job."

"Yes, girl!" Erykah exclaimed. "Homegirl over here juiced the hell out of Jessica and her daddy earlier this week for a bracelet and necklace. Got a good commission too."

"Well, shit. Keep pulling in that commission so we can keep having nights like this. Everybody knows that Jessica can't do shit like this if she doesn't have permission."

"Shut your mouth!"

"Permission?" Cherie quizzed.

"Girl, Shane got Jessica on such a tight leash that you would think she's choking by the time she makes it to her car. At first I thought that it was because she was pregnant… but now I think it's because he's somehow desperate. I don't know what the hell you put in his veins, but whatever. It's his life, I just hope she don't step out of line."

"Let's hope this growing up that Shane claims he's doing won't hurt her the way he hurt Cherie," Eykah added.

"What you mean?"

"Mandy told me that the bracelet I made for Shane with the halo on it was given back in a fuckin' envelope. You know I love my brother, but I disagree with some of the things that he's doing. Can't open my mouth about it because Shane tha God will make you feel real bad about yourself."

"Okay! Enough about Shane," Cherie intervened. "Ladies, I enjoyed you and enjoyed myself. Quita's right. We have to do this more often. Maybe next weekend we can invite Alyssa. That's her name, isn't it?"

"Yea, but Alyssa is sober now, so she might not want to drink. We can probably go to dinner or some shit."

"Yea, we can probably do that," Quita said. "I'm gonna introduce you to some of my homegirls in the near future. I know they would enjoy this shit."

"Hey, Quita, are you free on Tuesday between eleven and one?" Cherie asked her. "I need something different done to my hair."

"I'm sure I can squeeze you in. You enjoy the rest of your night and drive safely. I'll have Erykah text you my number." She leaned over and gave Cherie a hug before sliding into Erykah's Mercedes.

Erykah had given her a hug as well and demanded, "Eight tomorrow for the boutique. Saturdays, we open at noon and close at three, but I want you to be there early so I can show you some more stuff. Sundays, we're closed."

Cherie nodded and threw them a shy wave before she retreated to her Prius in the distance. When she reached it, a tall and chocolate god leaned against her driver's side door. A smile stretched over his face to show her his pearly whites.

"My condo... or yours?" he asked her.

"Yours," she giggled.

It was five in the morning when Shane came up for air. He whipped the covers back, away from him and Jessica and had to breathe for a moment. She sucked him, rode him, and threw her ass back when he had her bent over. He didn't know how much more he could take. She was wanting to go into early labor very badly, so sex was her only option. Shane had the package to achieve this, yet it wasn't working. She enjoyed the pain, though.

"Goddamn, Jessie," he said breathlessly. "We can't do that no more."

"Babe," she whined in between heavy breaths. She situated herself in bed and wrapped the flat sheet around her. "I'm still horny."

"You know I got things to do, Jessie. I would love to be here and help you to go into early labor, but I got to do a lot today."

"Like what, Shane?"

"Like helping Mama J get my daddy stuff together before they send him off to the hospital for hospice. And then I got to get to Quita's shop so she can change me up."

"When are you going to have time for me?"

"Come on, baby, you know I've been spending a grip of time with you, but I got to handle business. Ain't no compromise in it."

"Really? So, where all are you going today?"

"I just told you," he chuckled as he swung his feet over the edge of the bed.

"And who's all going to be with you?"

"Rich. Who else? I mean, Alyssa might come. She got a new job, I heard, so I'm not sure what her schedule is—"

"Don't play with me, Shane. Who else is going to be there?"

He got out of bed and stared at her. "What are you getting at, Jessica? Who else is supposed to be there other than Rich, possibly Alyssa, Bo and me?"

"Is Cherie going to be there?"

"Why the fuck…" He caught his words before he ripped her apart with them, and covered his mouth to make sure nothing would slip. She was making it real hard for him to do this whole growing up thing he was trying for so badly. "So… is this the reason you've been swinging around my neck so tough? Because she's in Virginia?"

"I know how you used to feel about her, Shane, so pardon me for being a skeptic and scared."

"You don't have shit to be afraid of. You have me. You know that."

"Well, she was a very intricate part of your life, and all of a sudden you're making changes. I was more comfortable when her ass was wherever she was." Angrily, Jessica whipped the covers off of her and scurried into the bathroom.

"If I wanted her, then I would've chased her! I would've had her," Shane bellowed, to make sure that his woman could hear him. "Jessie, me and her don't have a connection! What do I have to do to constantly prove that to you?"

"Nothing, Shane!"

"That's bullshit! I spend the majority of my days with you, and you're complaining about someone I hadn't seen or talked to?"

"*You* made me insecure because of her, so the only person you have to blame is yourself!"

Shane gritted his teeth and tried to swallow the fact that she was right, but she didn't have to come down hard on him.

"Did you know that she was working in Erykah's shop?" Jessica pulled the bathroom door open and stood there to glare at him. "I bet you they did that shit on purpose to make sure that you saw Cherie."

"You sound crazy right now," he said lowly. "Besides, how am I supposed to know who's working in my sister's shop? She didn't tell me. And obviously she didn't tell me for a reason, so don't trip on it."

"Whatever, Shane. You act like you don't care."

"I don't," he stressed. "What is important right now is what makes us happy, us having our baby soon, and finally sending my old man off."

"You wanna know what's going to make *me* happy?"

"For you to leave me alone about Cherie's ass. That would really make *me* happy. Somehow, you stopped thinking about that."

"Are you serious right now?"

"You know what I care about? Somebody finally making Shane happy. Jessica ain't doing that, and I gave you my all too. Please don't make me feel like you were a mistake."

"What?" she hissed.

"Look, take your shower," he said lowly. "I need to be meeting my mama. I gotta get ready to be out. We'll talk about this later. For once, I want someone to think of me."

"Shane—"

"I guess you got too comfortable, Jessica. Do you what you need to do, I got to go." He shook his head and went over to his closet to ready himself for the day. He couldn't believe that Jessica would have the audacity to bring something so stupid to him.

———

Quita was sitting in one of her chairs with her thick legs crossed while enjoying the gossip of the morning. She knew that when the clock struck nine her brother would be there, but for now, she was catching up on all the juice that one of her stylists' clients had about someone she knew. When the doorbell chimed and Shane tha God stepped into the place, no one was hushed. The only clients who had early appointments swooned at him and called out to him over how supposedly sexy he was. He ignored them and went to his sister's station.

She had gotten out of her seat and patted the headrest of it so that he could come and sit. He hiked up the dark blue denims he wore, and Quita noticed the Gucci band of green and red on the pocket of them, and took notice of his white t-shirt and Gucci shoes.

"No belt, no watch, no rings, no earrings, no necklace… just a bracelet," Quita commented as she started to take down the braids of his dreads that she had done before. "Either you were in a hurry to get the hell out of the house, or something is bothering you that much to when you put together this ensemble, you forgot to accessorize. My brother's a diva, but a manly one. He doesn't go without accessorizing shit. So what's good?"

"Jessica," he huffed. "She got this insane sense that I'm creepin' around with Cherie or some shit."

"Why the hell would she have that notion?" she laughed. "Hell, I ain't dropped by because Erykah told me that homegirl has this chip on her shoulder. What's going on?"

"The fuck if I know, Quita. I'm just gonna chuck it up to her having these pregnancy hormones or some shit. That's what I'm gonna say."

"She chewed you out this mornin'?"

"How did you know?"

"It's all over your face. You look frustrated. You know you can put a front on for everybody else, but you damn sure can't hide it from your sisters."

Shane looked up at her and noticed that she was wearing shades this early. "What the hell you get into last night?" he asked honestly.

"Chiiile! The question is what *didn't* I get into?"

"Y'all girls are wild."

"I truly enjoyed myself. To celebrate the new job, Cherie took me and Erykah to this club to see some strippers—"

"Cherie?" he questioned, looking up at her. "You say, club?... And you and Rick went with her?"

"Boy, shut up. We're all grown. Erykah complimented her on a job well done, straight out the gate, and we celebrated. It was such a breath of fresh air." She turned his head so that she could finish taking his braids down. "You ain't been worried about Cherie, so what's the deal now?"

"I'm gonna be honest with you and let you know that I ain't comfortable with this whole arrangement. When I break up with somebody, we all break up with them."

"Fool, she left *you*."

"So? That means she left this family."

"Shane, you don't seem to see everything like we do. Jessica got these little ways, and you're so blind to them that it's pitiful. She gets so full of herself that she makes herself look like an ass. I got to admit that I was wrong about Cherie. She's cool, down to earth, and the girl can let loose and have fun. Other than that, she got a new boo, so she ain't worried about your ass."

"What?" Shane leaned forward and contorted his neck to glare at his sister. "Fuck you mean—"

"Since I'm on a roll, let me let you know that Jessica is insecure as fuck. Maybe it's because of the thought of Cherie, or maybe not. But you keep on fuckin' with that girl, and she's gonna hurt you in the worst way possible."

As if hearing her name, the doorbell chimed and the curvaceous young woman stepped through with a pair of oversized shades on her face.

"Mmm." Quita twisted her lips up. "Go handle that before I forget her clingy ass is pregnant."

Shane rolled his eyes and traveled to the front of the shop to put out whatever argument was about ensue between him and the beauty.

Jessica walked out first and adjust the straps of her large purse on her wrist, then waited for him to settle down before she opened her mouth. "I'm going to be taking what little stuff that I have in the apartment, and I'm going back to my condo," she told him.

"For real, Jess?" His face scrunched at her statement. "You really want to do this because somehow you're insecure, after I've shown you that I'm only for you? You came all the way down here to try and hurt me to my face?"

"I'm not trying to hurt you, Shane. It's the simple fact that I have some issues that I need to work on. I've seen you bending over backwards for me. I was wrong to go off on you the way I did, and it made me think of why I was doing it. I just need some time to myself."

"You leavin' me?"

"No, baby," she whined. "I just want to get myself together. We have a baby coming in soon, and I don't want to spread you so thin by trying to be a father, a supportive brother, and keeping up with Apollo's business. Top it off, you'll have to try and please me. I don't want you to get tired of me and walk away because I can't control my temper, my feelings or my mouth. If you can do it, then so can I, alright?"

"You sure want this?"

"I'm sure, Shane." She rubbed his arm and gave him a small smile. "But… I promise you that by the time you carry me over the threshold of our new house, I'll be the one you need me to be."

"You know I love you, right, Jess?"

"I do."

He cradled her chin in his hand and kissed her full on the lips. "Don't work too hard," he grumbled when he pulled away. "Call me when you get settled. You know I'll be here for about four hours."

"I'll be done way before then," she giggled.

He gave her a playful pat on her backside before he turned away. Only, he turned away too soon. Shots rang out. Three that he could count, and he felt the sting of one on his arm. Tires screeched to get away from the front of the shop, and when Shane finally focused, he saw Jessica sprawled out onto the ground. Ignoring the pain in his arm, he dropped to his knees and screamed her name.

Quita rushed out of the broken glass door to see what was happening. "Shane!" she screamed.

"Call an ambulance!" he yelled back, without looking at her.

"Baby!" he cried, with her head in his lap. He rocked, but composing himself wasn't going to work. On the only day that he didn't take his piece out of the Jaguar was the day he regretted. His hand left her chest and smoothed down to her belly. Shane was cracking, and he didn't try to stop it. There was no hope in his mind that Jessica and the baby would pull through. Whomever pulled the trigger was probably dumb to the fact that this would make Shane either blood-thirsty... or break him completely.

CHAPTER NINE

Cue The Lightening

An hour prior...

Cherie didn't get any sleep the night before, and she and Damon decided to have a breakfast date. The vibe between them said that they had known each other for more than a week, yet they hadn't. They had a lot in common, including their love for laughter and the inner children that they were. Damon loved so much that she did, that it was ridiculous. She wondered where he was hiding when she had run into Terry for all of the wrong reasons. He made her forget about Shane and the hurtful things that he had said, Mandy turning her back on her own cousin, and everyone other than Erykah and Quita forgetting about her or acting like she didn't matter. With Damon, Cherie was lighter than a feather and she didn't have a worry. Unfortunately, she had to leave him and go to work. For lunch, they planned on meeting one another again.

She beamed when she read a text from him as Erykah opened the front door of the boutique.

Eykah had to roll her eyes at it. She already knew that Cherie was talking to her boo, but she didn't want to interrupt anything. "Got your nose wide open," she commented.

Cherie swayed into the boutique and headed to the back to place her purse down, then fidgeted with the end of her black chiffon cocktail dress to make sure that it was suitable. Her phone chimed and it was Damon, letting her know that he had an idea for their dinner date. She assured him that whatever he decided to do that she would be okay with that.

The doorbell to the boutique sounded off and it prompted Cherie to put her phone down on the single chair in the small room so that she could serve the first customer of the day, even though they weren't supposed to be servicing customers just yet.

"Welcome to Royal Six's," she said with a smile that all compliments of Damon in that moment. "How can I help you this morning?"

The thin, much older white woman looked up at Cherie's bright smile and said, "God, you're beautiful."

"Thank you," she giggled.

Suddenly, the woman's eyes fixed onto the exquisite jewelry that Cherie graced around her neck. "What's that on your neck?" she quizzed, almost transfixed on the expensive looking work.

Cherie looked down at the piece that she was wearing. Purposely, for the last week, she had been wearing pieces from the boutique and posting them on her new Instagram account, and giving the phone number and address to Royal Six's. This woman must've seen something that she posted recently. What she was wearing today was a silver chain link necklace that had pearls woven into them. She grazed her hand over the design with a grin on her face.

"This is a perfect combination between the metal and the pearls," Cherie began to sell the hell out of the piece that was worth $7,322. Her mind was on the commission and she was determined to get it. "The chain's links are silver, interwind with white nugget pearl that are freshwater and high quality. Don't let this innocent picture on my neck mislead you, though. This is a hand-made necklace that goes well with an evening gown for an impressive look, with a personal statement, to make any ex-husband pay for leaving you, or any young man want to flock to you because of your elegance."

"I see," the snooty woman hummed as she tapped her pointer finger against her chin. "Now, darling, I don't know what I want. My granddaughter saw a piece on your Instagram account. I believe you called it… the Heiress. Can I see that one?"

"Of course!" Cherie swayed over to the middle display and took the key from the secret square cut out from the floor to unlock the case, then pulled out a mannequin neck that held what the woman was searching for. On one of Cherie's lunch's, she pulled a lot of pieces and wore them, took pictures in them, and put them up on her Instagram. She was hoping that it would generate sales, and it did. Now she just had to inflate the price a little for the commission and benefit of the shop.

The 18-karat gold, curve link necklace connected at the buss with a 2-karat solitaire diamond. It made the older woman's mouth water.

"How much is this, dear?" she asked Cherie.

"$19,000," she answered right off. "The Heiress celebrates the elegance of femininity, creativity and craftsmanship. This necklace comprises large and luxe curb links for a style that is both on-trend and beautifully classic. In a nutshell... it fits you."

"Good. Give me both, the Heiress and that art from around your neck. I need them. I guess my granddaughter deserves a little treat as well, since she's the one who boasted over your post."

"Right away." Happily, Cherie went to Erykah's office and made a squished face at her. "I'm going to need two boxes," she informed her. "One for the Fresh Water that I have to take off... and the other for the Heiress."

Erykah's eyebrows raised as she stood from her seat. She hadn't even realized that Cherie was wearing her handcrafted design. That didn't matter at the moment. "You sold the Heiress?" she asked her, thoroughly impressed.

"Yep. And the Fresh Water."

"You? You sold the damn Heiress?"

"Yes," she giggled. "Now can you help me get out of this thing so I can clean it, box it and hope that this woman is going to want insurance on them both?"

"Whatever you say, honey. That's the largest damn commission anybody has made other than me." Erykah glided around her desk to help Cherie unclasp her necklace and personally took it to clean it.

Cherie had gone back to the front to collect the woman's payment information.

"Oh, darling, can you take a look at this ring for me?" the woman asked her. She stretched out her arm to show Cherie the rock on her finger. "Do you think it needs to be cleaned? It looks a little dull to me. What do you prefer?"

"To always shine brighter," Cherie grinned. "I'll take care of that for you too." Easily, she slipped the ring off of the woman's finger and made sure to add that to her bill. While Erykah was busy cleaning, she checked her phone to find a message from Damon. She smiled at the sweet gesture he pulled off when he told her not to work too hard and that he hoped that she had a good day.

After the transactions, Cherie sat on her stool and added pictures of her fingers in rings to her account. Erykah noticed it and all she could do was smile at her.

She sneaked up behind her and said, "So… I see you sellin' your ass off."

"You know it," Cherie giggled. "You told me that I had to earn commission, so that's exactly what I'm doing."

"Talked to your boo again?" she teased her as she eased up on a stool.

"Yea," Cherie sighed. "We're going to meet for lunch."

"You feelin' him?"

"I actually am," she confessed. "He makes me forget about everything, and I really do enjoy my time with him."

"You think it'll last?"

"I sure hope so."

Erykah pulled a key off her ring and handed to Cherie. "Your copy to the shop," she said. "And for the record... I have to be honest with you and say that I like to see you smile, but..."

"But what?" Cherie's smile slowly faded until there was nothing left. "Erykah, but what?"

"Fuck it. I'm gonna tell it like it is."

"Well, then, spill it."

"Cherie... I'm not really comfortable with the idea of you being with another guy."

"What?" Her face contorted and she could've cussed Erykah out for being so forward.

"Listen, it's not my life, so you don't have to listen to me. I mean, I had a damn blast last night. I really did. I started not to come in to the shop today because I'm kind of hungover, but that has nothing to do with what I'm trying to say."

"Then, can you get to it because I can't help but to feel slighted."

"This is stupid! You and Shane! This beef or whatever! I can't even believe he gives up on you after the way he talked about you for so many years. Girl, he talked about you like the second coming of Christ!"

"Shane has his ways, and so much came with him—"

"So, you're going to tell me that you're officially over him?"

"Where is this coming from?" Cherie hopped off the stool and placed her hand on her hip. "Seriously, Erykah! Shane wanted to move on, so that's what I'm doing. If he wanted me, then don't you think he would've put up with me too? The only reason I left Richmond was to clear my fuckin' name over some shit that I can't discuss. If Shane wasn't so damn selfish and would've been thinking of Cherie, then Shane would have Cherie. I had to step the fuck off. Where he's a good man, he's a dark one, and you won't understand that. No matter how long you and him have spent together, you will never be the one in the relationship that has to deal with him on a whole other level."

Erykah dropped her head and a smile spread onto her face.

"What's funny?" Cherie asked, offended.

"Jessica said the same damn thing about him before I hit her in the face… but in a completely different way."

"Well, it's true. He has this way about him that will make you fall in love with him, but then the other side will make you run for the damn hills."

"I get what you're saying, Rie, but I honestly don't think that either of you spent enough time to openheartedly hear one another out. I mean, you can't spend years apart and then snapback like nothing ever happened. Y'all have grown so much in that amount of time, and y'all rushed it. Mainly, my brother because as soon as he left the hospital from seeing my daddy, he sent out texts, telling everybody when they get to meet you. Now, I will say that the only reason he rushed back to Jessica was because you left, again. It was premature, and he was still searching for that love and affection that he thought that he was going to get from you."

"Erykah, none of that is my fault."

"I'm not pointing fingers. I'm just stating what I'm seeing from the outside and looking in."

Suddenly, Erykah's cellphone went off on her desk, and it was Quita's ringtone. She scrunched her brows and looked over her shoulder at it. She had Shane's head to do and two others at the same damn time. Why was she calling, Erykah wondered? She raised from stool and went to her phone in case her sister had been in some type of trouble, and answered.

"Quita—"

"Shane and Jessica were shot!" Quita rattled off. "Bitch, get here! I don't think Jessica is breathing!"

Erykah hung up and snatched up her purse from the floor. Without thinking of it, she scurried to the front door, forgetting that Cherie was even there. Her thoughts were all over the place, her body was numb and her bladder was threatening to relieve itself. She finally turned around and composed herself enough to say, "Cherie, Shane was shot—"

"What?" she shrieked. "I'm coming with you!"

"No! Stay here for the sake of the shop... and because I don't know what the hell is going on."

"Erykah, if something seriously happens to him—"

"I know, Rie! Alright! Just... please... stay behind. If he's in critical condition, then I will call you. I don't know what reaction he's going to give you. Besides, Jessica isn't breathing... at least Quita doesn't think she is. I don't want you to show up, and he flips the fuck out... but I promise I will keep you posted."

Without another word, Erykah was out of the building, leaving Cherie behind with tears finally falling. She began to pace until she went into the back to grab up her phone. She swiped past Damon's text and sent one to Shane, praying that he would reply just to say that he was okay.

It hit her like a ton of bricks to the chest that she wasn't over him. She wasn't going to be able to move on, because they still had unresolved issues and that it was almost too late to clear them. Cherie sat and grabbed at her curls, praying and wishing that Shane was okay and that the baby that Jessica was carrying would leave the earth before it even had a chance to see it.

CHAPTER TEN

In Rolls The Storm

It hadn't taken Shane long to have a doctor see him and remove the slug from his arm. He wasn't cooperative because he wanted to see Jessica and the baby, but the doctors were able to dig the hallow-point bullet out of his arm as much as they could so that they could get him out of the way. When he was stitched up and released, he tore through the first floor of the hospital, seeking answers. Shane couldn't take it anymore. He wasn't able to hold in the anger or the pain. He was like a rabid mongrel, foaming at the mouth with how he was shouting at nurses and doctors who passed him.

The Cruz women filed in to check on the brother, on the same day that their father had been admitted for hospice care, and the whole ordeal was so dark and gloomy. Even they wouldn't be able to contain him. Quita, Ash, and Alyssa ventured to their father's room, after hearing that Shane was no longer in surgery, just in case he had gone there after he left the first floor. Erykah, on the other hand, said to hell with everyone else. She was his ride-or die over everyone else, and she didn't care how long it took her to scour the hospital, she was determined to find her brother.

Finally, Shane was directed up to the fourth floor, and in the right direction. The same nurse who had given him the okay to proceed had made a call up to the nurses' station to let them know that he was coming and that he was crazed. A doctor received word and went into the hall after his work was done, to intercept Shane before he could punch holes into the room, or have security to come up to the fourth floor and drag him out of the building.

Erykah caught Shane on the fourth floor before he could do something crazy. She asked around for him, and the same nurse on the first floor had given her the same directions. She met with him while the doctor was explaining what had happened with Jessica. After the man in a white coat gave him the words that Shane didn't want to hear, everything changed. Shane couldn't hear a damn thing. All of the sounds in the busy hospital morphed into a distant whistle. Shane couldn't even blink or focus on the doctor's lips while he was giving Shane his condolences. The hairs on his arms and neck stood, and Shane's body had gone completely numb. So numb that he couldn't feel his weight give way.

Erykah ended up on her knees with her brother's head on her shoulder, while he let out body-trembling screams. She, herself, had to cry for him. How much did her brother have to take before he could get a decent break? It just wasn't fair. If she could defend him, she would, but from who or what?

He had to fight with himself to bring his head up. Shane didn't want to move. He didn't know how long he and Erykah sat together in the hall while the neckline of his shirt was being soaked. He couldn't even get his thoughts together. Out of all of the enemies that he was sure he made, Shane had one in particular that he couldn't get rid of. He blamed God. For some reason, the higher being hated him and kept stripping him of happiness every time it came around to him. His leg danced as people passed. Even though he knew that he wasn't alone, he still felt that he was. Erykah's soft hand on his back wasn't doing anything for him.

The only upside was that Shane could go to the NICU in a few hours to see the little one that they saved before it was too late.

"Mr. Hartford?" a nurse lowly called to him. "You have someone to meet in the NICU," she said sweetly.

Had it not been for Erykah, he wouldn't have been able to get up and go to the elevator, or walk a line just to see who he and Jessica had created. As soon as he stopped at the glass container and laid eyes on the little face, and saw the tube stretching up her nostril, Shane collapsed onto his knees again.

Erykah wrapped her arms around her brother and squeezed him. "She's a girl, Shane," she whispered. "You got to name her, brother."

"Get me out of here," he struggled to say. The majority of his sentence was filled with air.

His sister obliged, even though she didn't want to. Lucky for them that Josiah, Jessica's father, was called by the hospital, and they hadn't run into him when they there, or else they would've never gotten Shane off the floor.

In the drive-thru of Walgreen's, Erykah surfed through her phone at the million questions that had come through about Jessica. She was waiting for her brother's medicine and had nothing better to do. She hated to see Shane so broken and weak, but had she opened her mouth, she wouldn't get a response from him. She didn't want to push him.

"*Is everything alright with Shane and Jessica?*" Cherie asked via text.

"*Waiting on his meds now, but it's so much going on and I'm hurt and scared,*" she replied. "*Shane ain't okay, and Jessica didn't survive. It's pretty dark in that head of his, and it doesn't take a rocket scientist to know what's going to happen next.*"

"*Do you think he would want to see me?*"

"*I don't advise that. Do me a favor and close up shop. You can have the rest of the day off.*"

"*I will. Let me know if he needs anything.*"

Erykah didn't bother to reply. She retrieved her brother's medicines and took him home.

"Take me to the big house," he said hoarsely, as soon as his sister had gotten onto the freeway.

"What?" she asked curiously. "Why would you go there? No one's there."

"I need to be alone," he choked. "I can't deal, Erykah."

"Shane, I'm not leaving you by yourself."

"It's not a time to argue with me. Just, please... I... I can't, right now." Shane sniffled, still trying to hold on to the last of his sanity. "You don't know! You don't know how the fuck it feels not being able to breathe, while you're breathing. You don't know what it feels like to lose and gain… to lose and gain… and to lose and fuckin' gain, because that's exactly what's happening! I gotta always pretend every-fucking-thing is okay! I gotta be Apollo's son! I got to be the best there ever was, and since my *daddy* never cracks, then I'm not allowed to! You don't how it feels to be in a room full of fuckin' people, just to be alone, Rick! You don't know! You damn sure don't know how it feels to have everybody you love to be taken away from you, like you're cursed; you're being punished for something…" The tail end of his sentence was nothing but air with an odd combination of a squeal.

Erykah swallowed the feeling of wanting to shake him. She feared for him. She knew that he shouldn't have been alone at a time like this, but she had no choice for the sake of argument. She dropped him off, with his medicines, and called her mother, Bo, and Rich. They already had wind of what was happening, yet no one decided that it was fitting to go to the house before she dropped him off. A part of her felt torn. She wanted to be there for her brother, but she had to be there for her father as well. Someone was going to have to be there, in a physical sense, for Shane. On a whim, she sent Cherie a text that told her that she needed her to find the Cherie that Shane loved. She was going to have to pull something out of her that he needed from her. She was scared that it wouldn't work, but if anyone could stand to see Shane in the state he was in, and would've been able to coach him through the pain, she wholeheartedly felt that it would've been Cherie.

Shane, on the other hand, heard voices of doubt and anger. He waddled up the stairs, taking his sweet time. His bones and heart were all heavy, and he just couldn't take anymore. The precious little girl that was a miracle for the doctors to recover was doomed, he thought. To have a father like him, she wasn't supposed to be attached. If she was, she was bound to die too. It all made sense to him. His mother, his father, Jessica, all fell victim. The baby had just gotten here. He felt as if he had to save her. The only way he could do that was to open his medicine bag of pain killers and swallow as much as he could. It was to put a stop to all of the pain his heart, the guilt, the death, the sorrow and the confusion. Somehow, this made sense to him, so it was ethical.

On the flipside, he didn't want her to be angry with him if she grew up without him. She wanted him to know what had happened and why he had to leave her so soon. He found a notepad in the drawer of his nightstand and penned an open letter to her, not even realizing that he was going to have to name her in order to do so.

Miracle,

> *Believe me or not, I love you. I don't want you to ever think that this isn't true. Your daddy has some type of curse, demon, or witch riding his back, and it's taking everything away from him. One by one, everyone that I love is dropping and being covered in the earth. If not that, then they just leave. This includes your mother. I want to tell you how sorry I am…*

A teardrop splashed onto the last letter and left it as an oblong shape on the white page. He sniffled and continued. He was much lower than low and couldn't take the weight of the darkness anymore. After pushing himself through the letter, he signed it, dated it, and swallowed ten pills that he could count. It had finally happened. Shane broke. He was hopeless and helpless.

CHAPTER 11

Happened To Me

Hurriedly, Cherie closed the shop when she had the green light and received the text from Erykah to be at Shane's side. She knew how important Apollo was to them all, but that was no excuse for no one to be there for Shane. Maybe Erykah wanted to give him the happiness he had been searching for, and use Cherie to plug the hole in the dam that broke within Shane's emotions and his mental instability. Erykah had hoped that Cherie could throw on whatever cape that she used to wear in order to get the job done.

Cherie's cheeks were glistening while she was trying to get her keys together to get into the car. Then, her trembling and shaking fingers wouldn't allow her to enter the address to the Big House so that she could go there. She had to stop and get herself together; piece herself together so that she could leave. When she pulled away from the parking lot of the boutique, her eyes were cloudy and her mind was racing. This time, she made sure to properly dry her eyes so that she wouldn't have a reoccurrence of what had happened weeks ago with the Tesla. Her phone, on the passenger seat, startled her.

She picked it up without looking at the display. "Hello?" she answered with a shaky voice.

"Hey, Rie," Damon nervously greeted her. "You don't sound okay. Is everything alright?"

"Umm… yea," she lied. "I just have to check on an old friend. That's all. It's just been very dramatic, and I'm really trying to get it together…" She took a deep and unexpected breath against her will.

"Babe… you don't sound alright. You sound like your aura is in disarray. Do you have enough time to meditate?"

"I wish I did," she sniffled.

"Okay, well I'm going to need for you to focus on your breathing while you're driving, okay? If not, you're going to panic, your heartrate is going to shoot through the roof, and you might even end up passing out. Can you keep it cool for me this one time? Please?"

"Damon—"

"Cherie, I understand that you're doing this for your friend, but I don't know them. I'm getting to learn you. My priority is you. So imagine what it's going to be like you manage to wreck or fall out somewhere? I'm not sure how I would react to that, honestly. Besides, your friend needs you right now, and you can't be there for someone if you aren't there for yourself."

She was pleased with everything he had said. Cherie had never had anyone to be there for her when she truly needed them to be. It proved that Damon was one hell of a force to be reckoned with if it was going to be a battle in her mind between him and Shane, but even that was at the back of her mind.

"Promise me that you're going to breathe this thing through."

"I will," she returned, much stronger than before.

"Alright. Call me and keep me posted alright?"

"Yes, Damon."

"I care about you, Cherie."

"I care for you too." Her eyes welled again after he hung up. This was going to be harder than she thought.

Damon was a good guy, but what she shared with Shane was one force that couldn't be explained or pinpointed. She was being pulled into two different directions. She wanted to be there for her friend, but there was the risk of losing someone so promising. She wanted to turn around and run into Damon's arms, just to get off the merry-go-round that was her situation with Shane. It was so strong that she looked at three exits very closely as she drove past them on the freeway, contemplating on claiming some sort of freedom that she wasn't sure that she wanted or needed at the time.

"We're not selfish," she coached herself, as she mashed the gas a little harder so that she could make it to the Big House under the time that the GPS told her that she would be there.

––––––––

Cherie had gotten out of the Prius and sent Damon an apology text, letting him know that she was going to have to cancel their lunch and dinner plans. Purposely, she waited for his reply, and she had gotten back what she expected of him. He was sweet and understanding, and opted to reschedule whenever need be. It was a sacrifice that she was willing to make.

Cautiously, she approached the double doors and opened one, with the feeling of dread washing over her. "Shane!" she called. "Hello?" She took her time to ease up the stairs and chose to turn to the left instead of right.

She noticed, on the doors, that there were names engraved into the cherry wood. By the time she reached the end of the hall and saw the blazing sun that was etched inside the double doors, she knew that she had the wrong room. Quickly, she pattered down the hall to check the names on the other side until she was face to face with the "De'Shane—The Prince" on the front of the glossy door. She turned the gold doorknobs.

"Cherie!" she heard, and it startled her. "Shane?"

She whirled around and screamed, "Rich! I'm up at Shane's room!" Without telling him anything else, she forced herself into Shane's massive bedroom and gasped at what was in front of her.

She rushed to a sprawled out Shane on the floor, with his legs in a figure four, and in his hand was a letter. She pulled it out of his hand and sat it on the couch that he lay in front of. "Shane?" she cried his name as she shook him lightly. "Shane! Can you hear me?"

Rich's sneakers squeaked when he slid into the room. But as soon as he looked down at Shane, he caved. "Oh, come on, bruh!" he panicked and whisked over to the pair on the floor.

Cherie checked for a pulse, and Rich moved her hand out of the way to drag him over to the bed. Cherie helped by pulling Shane's feet over the starched covers.

"Cherie, call an ambulance," he demanded.

She searched around the room until she located a phone on the other side of his bed, hurried over to it, and snatched it up. With vibrating fingers, she called the emergency support and waited for someone to answer.

"Shit," Rich cursed under his breath. He started chest compressions on Shane and it made Cherie panic worse than what she was.

"Nine-one-one, what's your emergency?" the woman on the other end asked.

"Yes, umm... m-m-my name is Cherie, and my... m-m-my friend collapsed," she stammered.

"Is your friend breathing, ma'am?"

"No, he's not. My other friend has begun chest compressions."

"Does your friend that collapsed have a pulse?"

"Yes, he does. It's very light. It's almost like a flutter."

"Does friend take medications? High blood pressure or diabetes?"

Cherie scanned the room to see what the hell Shane could've strangled himself with or what he tried to knock himself out with at least. "N-n-not that I know of, now. He's a very healthy eater." Then, she spotted the open pill bottle on the arm of the couch, and her worst fears were confirmed. Shane tried to kill himself. "He... h-h-he took pills. I'm not sure how many."

"I'm sorry?"

"*Pills*! He swallowed pills out of a bottle!"

"How long has your friend been performing these chest

compressions, ma'am," the woman asked calmly.

"Since just before you answered the call."

"Okay. Hang on and we'll get someone out to you as soon as possible."

Cherie hung up, tossed the phone and went to the letter. She briskly folded it and stuffed it into her bra. Afterward, she moved Rich over, straddled Shane, and pushed her palms into his chest as hard as she could. So hard that his head was jerking over the pillow below him.

"Fuck that," she mumbled as she was damn near driving a hole into his chest. "You don't get to cheat. Hell no. If I have to stay here, you got to stay with me, motherfucker. Come on, Shane. Breathe. *Breathe*, you demented fucker." She then leaned down and pressed her ear against his chest to listen for his heartbeat. "No," she said aloud. "You don't get to leave." Again, she pumped into his chest until she pinched his nose, tilted his head back, and gave him breaths that she was hoping would help him to breath on his own.

"Rie—"

"Shut up, Rich!" she screamed with tears that she ignored falling down her cheeks. She pumped Shane's chest some more, then gave him longer breaths. She wasn't going to give up on him. "Get up, Shane!" She yelled like a mad woman.

Rich reached for her, but he ended up pulling away, as Shane sprung up from the mattress and spewed his stomach contents all over Cherie's bosom. As quickly as he rose, Shane slammed into the bed and gagged and coughed. More fluid overflowed out of his mouth, but Cherie hadn't been afraid of it. She remembered when her mother tried to overdose with pills. She had to work on Shane the same way she did with Davetta.

"Rich, go and get me some milk," she alerted him as she climbed off of Shane.

Rich didn't ask any questions. He flew out of the room like the backs of his shoes were on fire.

Cherie pulled Shane by his arm to make him roll over onto his stomach, and repositioned him so that his head was hanging off of the bed. Finally, she pushed against his back and repeated the chest compressions, only they weren't on his chest. They were in the middle of his back to make his stomach churn at the motion of the bed. She had to get him to throw up everything he had swallowed.

Rich had come back into the room with a gallon of milk in his hand, and waited for Cherie to turn Shane over onto his back. She snatched the gallon out of his hand and unscrewed the top.

"Now, I'm gonna pour this into his mouth," she explained. "When he chokes, turn his head to the side so that he doesn't drown, so that he can spit it out."

"Is this gonna—"

"We don't have time for you to be a pussy!" she yelled at him. Without giving him a warning, she poured the milk into Shane's mouth, and Rich waited for him to gag.

When he did, Rich turned his chin and stood back so that Shane could puke. Shane, himself, lazily reached over and turned onto his stomach. He kept spilling his stomach contents until there was streaks of red in in the fluid.

"He's straining," she panicked. She put the gallon on the floor and rushed over to him to get him to sit up.

"Paramedics!" they heard.

Rich backwards jogged out of the room with his eyes still on his old friend, so that he could lead the first responders up to the room.

Cherie help him up with his arm over her shoulder and her left hand pressed into his chest.

Lazily, he opened his eyes and tried to focus on her. "Rie," he called her no higher than that of a whisper. "What you doin' here?"

"Saving you," she harshly said.

"We're late for school," he mumbled. Then, his eyes rolled into the back of his skull and they both fell over onto the bed.

Rich rushed the paramedics into the room and helped Cherie off the bed. "Let them work, and you change clothes," he urged her.

Without thinking of it, she moved as quickly as she could to rummage through Shane's drawers to find a t-shirt and a pair of gym shorts. Afterward, she scurried into the bathroom in the room, stepped out of her dress and heels, and grabbed a black wash cloth off the basin to wet it and drown it in Old Spice that was conveniently placed along the basin to ceiling mirror. Cherie had never washed up so quickly in her life. Her body was still a little damp when she slipped into the clothes that she grabbed, but she didn't care about that. Lastly, she pulled the crumpled letter up off the floor and stuffed it into the pocket of the shorts so that she could read it at another time. In less than four minutes, she was back inside the room, watching them place Shane on a stretcher.

"W-w-where are they going?" She nervously asked Rich, who had the nail of his thumb inside his mouth.

He looked over at her with a worried expression and a look of sorrow in his eyes. "They have to take him in," he said as calmly as he could.

"Then you grab my phone and purse out of my car, and I'll ride with them."

He nodded and sprinted out of the room. Cherie was close on his heels so that she could meet the paramedics in the back of the rig.

Once they loaded Shane, the only thing that Cherie had to do was grab her phone from Rich and stuff it into her pocket. She anxiously waited for them to close the door and to get the rig moving so that they would give her the okay that Shane would pull through.

The paramedics had the chance to cut open Shane's polo and slap stickers onto his chest, connect the portable EKG machine, and found a very faint heartbeat. Cherie ignored what the paramedics were saying to one another. Her focus was on Shane as he lay there on the stretcher limp. They tried everything to get him to breathe, but nothing was working. Cherie's heart dropped with the EKG machine went flat.

EPILOGUE

Without Us

11 Years Ago...

"*T*ogether, we got plenty of power," Shane chuckled, with his eyes on his runover Chuck's. He was walking along the railroad tracks, almost a mile away from their block. He and Cherie weren't supposed to be there, but they were, and they knew that they would have their skin handed to them if they were found off their grounds. "Girl, you ain't got nothin' to be scared of."

"You don't understand, do you, Shane?" She questioned, scratching at the zig-zag cornrows that Mandy had put in her auburn hair that she hated. Her cousin was just learning how to braid and Cherie's hair was a mess. She just didn't have the heart to tell her cousin that she wouldn't make it into beauty school with crooked parts and different sized braids. "Without you, I feel like I'm nothing! And now, my mama wants me to move clear across the country, away from you. I'll die out there, you hear me? Shane, I would *diiiie*!"

"You're so dramatic," he laughed. Shane hopped off the steel beam and laid his hands on her waist, looking right into her eyes so that she would receive the message loud and clear, and hope that she understood him. "You think that I'm gonna be okay without you?"

"Yes," she said smartly as she worked her neck.

"Well, then, you're so wrong that you couldn't be more *wrongerer.*"

"That's not a real word. That doesn't make any sense."

"That's how wrong you are, Rie." He winked and smirked at her.

"I'm weak! The world is going to eat me up and swallow me whole out there. I wish you could just fit yourself inside a briefcase or something."

"Yea, and how about I mail myself to your new house? Nothing says best friendship like springing up out of a box on your mama to give her a heart attack."

"At least she'd die, and I would be free by then."

"I think you're being a little too hard on yourself."

Too much was going through her mind. She just knew that she was doomed. She looked around for a moment before she could grasp her surroundings. She knew that it was a small body of water on the other side of the tall grass, so she did the only thing that was going to set her free. Cherie moved away from Shane and walked a few feet away to pick up a couple of stones from the side of the train tracks. She quickly stuffed them into the pockets of her short overalls and took off running as fast as she could when she could fit no more inside. Because of the weight of the stones in her pockets, it slowed her down a little.

Shane was able to catch her before she could step on the marshland on the other side of a gate of tall grass.

He grabbed her arms and fell back on his ass with how hard he snatched her.

"Let me go, Shane!" she screamed as she wiggled out of his grasp. The two engaged in a slap-boxing match before either of them could get up.

"No! You're being stupid!"

"No, I'm not!" She succeeded at freeing herself. It took her a moment to stand with the weight of the stones in her pockets, but she regained her balance and looked down at him with her chest heaving.

"Your last resort is to kill yourself?"

"So?" she screeched.

"Ay, yo! You stupid as fuck right now, Rie!"

"How? I don't want to be here! Were you not listening? Davetta can't make me go anywhere if I'm dead! That makes *perfectly* good sense, right?"

"Fuck *her*, Cherie, I need you!"

"You don't need me, Shane. You got thick skin. You got fire, you got spunk, and you got vigor. What I got? *Nothin'*! That's what's gonna get me killed out here if I don't do it myself." She folded her arms over the chest of her overalls and pouted. "At least that'll take away some of the satisfaction of someone else doing it."

Shane got off the soft earth, finally, and grabbed Cherie's arm to pull her into him. "Listen to me, okay? It doesn't matter where you go,

I'll always be there!"

"You don't see the way that man looks at me, Shane," she cried. "If he don't kill me physically, he's gonna do it mentally, emotionally... He's gonna kill me from the inside out. I know so."

He took a deep breath and brought them both down onto the ground on their knees. With her shoulders sandwiched between his palms, he rested his forehead on hers. "Rie, it doesn't matter what they do to our bodies," he grumbled. "I'm always I'm going to be in here." He slowly and carefully swayed his hand down from her shoulder and placed it over her heart. Then, he took hers away from her thigh and pulled one of her hands over his own heart. "Just like you're going to be in here. And it doesn't matter how cold or hard they might try to make our hearts, or how they may break them... we'll always be here." Gently, he guided her hands up to either side of his forehead and rested his on her face, with her ears between his index and thumbs. "Promise me. Promise me that you won't forget."

"I... I ca—"

"Say it, Cherie," he lowly demanded.

"I promise," she sniffled.

"Now promise me that you'll come back. I don't care if you run away when you're sixteen and hop state lines. Promise that you're going to come home."

"I promise."

Satisfied with their verbal agreement, Shane stood and helped her up. Together, they removed the stones from her pockets and continued their journey to nowhere in particular before dusk approached.

"What is this?" she asked honestly. "What is this thing that's between us? How do you have the power just to calm me down?"

"I don't know, Rie," he shrugged. "Maybe we're too young to understand right now, but it's strong, whatever it is."

She took her eyes up to his, and they were filled with hope. He could see it. "Do you love me?"

"Yes," he answered right off. "Whatever the hell this thing is between us lets me know that. What about you?"

"Do I know that I love you?" she quizzed.

"Yea. Do you?"

"Yes," she blushed.

"How do you know?"

"Because if it was you with stones in your pocket, trying to drown yourself, I would've kept you from jumping in the water too."

"Well, there we go then."

"But, Shane?"

"Yea?" He kicked a rock and watched the distance of it before he turned to her. "What?"

"Would you die for me?" she suddenly asked.

"No," he answered. "I wouldn't try to leave you by yourself like that. That's a bitch move. If I leave, half of you would be gone, girl. Why you think I wouldn't let you off yourself? Because half of me would be gone too."

"Has anybody told you that you're crazy?" she giggled.

He grabbed up her hand and laced their fingers. "Plenty of times, but you know what?"

"What?"

"I'm only crazy for you."

"We're kids!" she stressed with a smile.

"That's what we *want* them to believe."

She shrugged and kept along their walk while her wheels were still turning. "What if I don't ever come back?"

"Then I'll come and find you."

"You're going to find someone else, I'm sure."

"Like I said, it's something here that we can't explain. If it gets stronger with age, I'm sure that you'll never be replaced."

"What if we can't figure out how to get me back?"

"I'm sure we'll figure something out, Rie. You think too much." He let go of her hand and pulled her head into his shoulder. "No matter what though, I'm always going to be there. You can count on it."

TO BE CONTINUED

Looking for a publishing home?

Royalty Publishing House, Where the Royals reside, is accepting submissions for writers in the urban fiction genre. If you're interested, submit the first 3-4 chapters with your synopsis to submissions@royaltypublishinghouse.com.

Check out our website for more information:

www.royaltypublishinghouse.com.

Text ROYALTY to 42828 to join our mailing list!

To submit a manuscript for our review, email us at
submissions@royaltypublishinghouse.com

Text RPHCHRISTIAN to 22828 for our
CHRISTIAN ROMANCE novels!

Text RPHROMANCE to 22828 for our
INTERRACIAL ROMANCE novels!

Do You Like CELEBRITY GOSSIP?

Check Out QUEEN DYNASTY!
Visit Our Site: www.thequeendynasty.com

Get LiT!

Download the LiTeReader app today and enjoy exclusive
content, free books, and more